THE PRESIDENTS' DAUGHTERS

FRONT AND CENTER

STEFNE MILLER

THIRTY ACRE WOODS

ACKNOWLEDGMENTS

Thank you to everyone who help make this series possible!

Developmental Edits: Dawn Alexander (Evident Ink)

Line Edit: Sonya Barker Editing Services

Cover Design: Lacy Skrapka (Hope Graphics)

Audio Book Narration: Kahlie Metz

Blurb/Synopsis: Nancy Smay (Evident Ink)

GRAB THE PRESIDENTS' DAUGHTERS SERIES "BIBLE"

Sign up for Stefne Miller's newsletter to receive your free copy of the series "bible".

One read-though of the is series bible and you'll be fully prepared to dive into the world of Tucker-Grace, Fiona and Jack.

http://grassroots.fashion/updates

GRASSROOTS. FASHION

Hello, world!

Welcome back to Grass Roots Fashion where we step into Fiona Wright's campaign closet and use her eye-popping style to inspire affordable looks all our own (and meet at the clothesline to share a little gossip along the way).

Guess where I am?

Believe it or not, I'm at the National Presbyterian Church over on Nebraska Avenue in DC and camped out with a throng of Quaid Wright supporters.

If you've never been here, this place is stunning.

The kind of church that politicians like to attend because it's so beautiful, carries a lustrous history and looks great in photos. I bet most attend regularly during election season.

Not the Wrights, though. I'm sure they attend year-round. They aren't the type to do things just for show.

When their entourage pulled up, I shoved my way to the front and got a good look at the family as they walked into the building for service but was heartbroken when I realized that Jack wasn't with them. (Scoop on why on the Clothesline below.)

The Vice-President, Second-Lady, and Fiona graciously waved to us as they walked in but didn't stop to say hello. Now, we're all waiting around hoping that when the service ends, they'll reward us with a few words and time for photos.

And now, the reason we're all here, — Fiona.

The Closet:

She looked spectacular. Of course.

Simple. Elegant. Comfortable.

And believe it or not, it's a look that a lot of us might actually be able to afford!

As I'm sitting here waiting for them to walk out of the building, I did my research and found her dress. It's a ruffled summer dress by Michael Kors (of course — he's her favorite designer), and the sea coral color really stands out against her beautiful skin.

With her fabulous eye for fashion, Fiona paired the dress with simple, jute wrapped nude wedge that added a good three inches to her already tall frame.

The dress hit her a little above the knee, and a live

glimpse of her legs is enough to make me want to take up track. Unbelievable.

A word to the wise and all hardcore Fiona fans, if you get the chance to see this family live while they're on the campaign trail, DO IT! They're amazing to see on television or online but to see them live and in person, well — they're magnificent.

To see their wardrobe head over to my post at: https://www.grassroots.fashion/post/fiona-s-cathedral-attire

The Clothesline:

Make this a combo of the latest Clothesline gossip and The Swoon because this scoop is about our boy, Jack.

This morning I got word that he was seen at Bluxom last night. Yes, that Bluxom. The bar Jack is too young to enter, Bluxom.

He arrived with an entourage of friends from All Saints High, but it didn't take long before he and a gorgeous red-head disappeared into a curtained off private room, and nobody saw them again for the rest of the night.

Typical Jack Wright behavior. But don't we still love our bad boy?

If this story is true, Jack may not be praying at church because he's praying to the porcelain god at home. ;)

The Wrap:

Before this election cycle, I didn't even know what a red, blue or purple state was. And for those of you like me, red leans Republican, blue leans Democrat, and purple is a toss-up or in this case, we're hoping, Indy)

But now that I'm more in the know and have taken to this amazing family, I'm Quaid Wright all the way!

Okay, back to waiting for them to walk out. I'll catch all of you grassroots girls later!

2

FIONA

I'M small compared to the substantial National Presbyterian Church Cathedral.

While under normal circumstances, I would blend into the crowd and go unnoticed, my life isn't normal, and all eyes are on my parents and me.

We didn't wave to the people who turned in their pews to watch us enter and walk down the aisle to our own row of seats. If we did, it would make it appear that this is a campaign event. But this isn't an event; it's church. A time to rest and reflect.

For the next hour, I can finally focus on something other than politics or fashion. I can breathe.

I'm sitting between my father and mother on the wooden bench and am trying hard to focus on the pastor's message, but my parents simultaneously pulled their phones out and are frantically scrolling through messages.

Trying not to be obvious, I reach down like I'm going to scratch my leg, reach into my purse and retrieve my cell phone. Like theirs, notifications fill my home screen.

Wright Selects Running Mate

Will We Finally Have a Female Vice-President?

My chest tightens as I continue to scroll.

A Single Mother May Soon Be the Most Powerful Woman in the Country.

Josephine Bishop. Her name is familiar. I've heard my parents and their staff discuss her but didn't know they finalized a decision.

I tilt my phone to the left so my father can see the notifications, then look up at him, hoping he can read my confusion on my face.

He smiles and nods, certain that all eyes are on us, then looks down. I follow his line of sight and see both of his palms up, in a slight shrug of the lower half of his arms.

The slight shrug implies that he's as confused by the announcement as I am. I nod.

My father wraps his arm over my shoulder and pulls me closer while he simultaneously places his hand on my mother's shoulder.

We're in this together, and he's bracing us for an onslaught of questions as soon as the service comes to a close.

My stomach churns. I lean closer to my father, try to calm my nerves, and wish I could calm his.

I'm certain this news has left him reeling. My father and his campaign staff take every precaution to move slowly and with perfectly calculated steps. They weren't going to schedule to announce for several more weeks.

In campaigns, timing is everything, and the timing is off.

As the pastor continues, I'm left to sit in near agony and wait until we can figure out how this mishap will affect the campaign, and my family's future.

3

JACK

Sleep is not my friend.

At least not when a beam of light is shining through an opening of the curtains hanging in my window. I glance at my phone and see it's past noon, which is late. Even for me.

My head is pounding, and my mouth is dry. I didn't drink enough to cause either and drank a ton of water before we went out. I'm sluggish. The fog that smothers you when you sleep for too long.

There are two knocks on the door. And a third.

One. Two. Three. Four.

On cue, Tanner charges into the room. "Get up, Jack." He's in a foul mood again. "They'll be heading back soon."

I groan and cover my head with my pillow.

"I am a college educated political mind, not a freaking babysitter. I said get up!"

He's also a toady, bowtie wearing man-boy who suffers from short-man syndrome. I still can't figure out how my dad thought he would be the best choice to be my handler.

His feet pound the floor as he strides across the room. He

yanks the curtains open, sliding them across the rod with a scrape. "I couldn't hate this job any more if you stuck me at Gitmo."

"You can leave anytime." I throw the pillow onto the floor and pull the covers from my face but am immediately blinded by the sunlight. "Did you need to do that?"

"No, and you sound like you smoke three packs of cigarettes a day. Or drank too much last night. I'm guessing it's both."

"Your confidence in me is inspiring." But given my past, I can't blame him for the assumption.

I've never liked the guy. He's one of those who went to a top college and believes that should have earned him a high-paying job, a big house and a sports car — all within months of graduating. In reality, he's a low-level staffer living in a loft with four other low-level staffers and sharing a Lyft to work every day.

In other words, he's in hell. I don't have sympathy for him. In DC, people rarely get what they deserve. The people who act the worst, accomplish the most, so knowing he's living his own personal nightmare, makes seeing the trash of DC succeed, lessen the sting.

"You're expected downstairs for brunch," he barks.

"Already?" I roll onto my back, shove another pillow from my bed under my head and wipe my tired eyes. "I was out of it."

I stretch my legs, kick something beside me in the bed, and yank my leg back. A muffled sigh under the sheets catches me off guard. I must not have slept alone last night and without even remembering who, I regret it.

The pounding between my ears intensifies. My headache now throbs.

"What's her name?"

I stare at the lump in the covers trying to remember her. Her name isn't coming to me. "Um…"

"Ava," she says, from under the covers.

"Right. Ava."

Tanner picks her clothes up off the floor and flings them onto the bed. "Ava?"

We wait. Ava removes her head from under the covers, and her red hair releases a brief memory of her joining my friends and me at the back of the bar. The drinks started flowing not long after she sat down beside me. I liked her red hair and the fact that she wasn't a student at All Saints.

"Your time here is over," Tanner says through the bathroom door. "You've got to go."

I throw the comforter off. I've still got my jeans on from the night before, at least confirming that I didn't do anything too stupid last night.

After grabbing a T-shirt off the drum stand, I pull it on as Ava slips out of the bed, surrounds herself in the bedsheet, slides off the bed, and runs into the bathroom. Her red hair is so long it covers her bra strap and reaches the top of her underwear.

"What happened to discretion?" Tanner whispers as soon as the bathroom door shuts.

I scratch my head and look around the room, frustrated that I don't remember more about bringing her back home. "I don't remember her coming here, to be honest."

Tanner crosses his arms and looks at me. "Of course not."

"I had one drink."

Tanner places his hands on his hips and inspects my room with a scowl. "All eyes are on you, Jack. You're now in a fishbowl. Remember that." He lowers his voice. "Your father's VP choice got leaked this morning. He's flying her in for a meeting." He peers around again and shakes his head. "She'll be here at four. Get this place cleaned up so I can send a maid in here to vacuum and dust." He sniffs three times. "And spray some disinfectant."

Ignoring his command to clean my room, I stand and stagger towards my desk, picking up a drumstick as I pass. "How did that happen?" I yawn. "The leak."

"You know DC, nothing stays secret around here." Tanner turns to the bathroom door. "Ava! Get out here. We've got to escort you off the premises. Trust me, you don't want to meet the Vice President under these circumstances."

I'm sure my dad already knows about my guest, and he will be angry with me whether or not he catches sight of her. But Tanner's right. It wouldn't be fair to her to put her in such an uncomfortable situation. Intentional on my part or not.

It's best if she's long gone before everyone returns.

I open my computer and go to a website to check the latest news. Sure enough, Tanner was right. My dad's choice of a running mate is top of the screen news.

While Tanner paces the room waiting for the girl, I check several more sites. All of them claim their sources told them Josephine Bishop was my dad's choice for Vice-Presidential candidate.

After too many minutes, Ava opens the bathroom door, but I don't look back at her. I hate moments like this. When a girl stays the night without invitation and then expects a long, drawn-out goodbye and promises of seeing each other again.

"Thanks for such a good time," she says.

I wave over my shoulder and continue to read the news about Josephine Bishop, the single mother from Texas.

"Let's go, Ava," Tanner says. "You can pick up your phone at the security gate."

"Oh. I have it right here."

My fingers tense over the keyboard at my colossal screw up of allowing her inside with the phone still in her possession and sense Tanner is probably glaring at the back of my head.

"Of course, you do," he snaps.

"We should do this again," Ava offers. "Soon."

"Yeah, okay." I check out the other leading stories while Tanner is tasked with removing Ava from the premises with as much discretion as he can manage.

Come to think of it, I'd hate my job too if I were him.

Relieved that Ava is almost gone, and Tanner's doing the dirty work, I check over my shoulder to make sure Tanner has left and shut the door behind him. I figure it'll take him at least five minutes to deliver Ava to the security gate, get her in a vehicle, and see her off the property. I enter the private chat room that I check several times per day.

As expected, there's a message waiting for my attention. Got your scoop about Josephine Bishop. Leaked it this morning. Anything new?

I respond: Meeting between V.P. and Ms. Bishop at four. Location: VPR.

Vice President's Residence.

I sit back in the chair and stare at my message.

I don't enjoy being a rat, but a rat is what they raised me to be. Sometimes I like it, but more often than not, I end up regretting poorly thought out behavior like what I did last night and what I'm doing every day now by leaking information.

I press <enter> and immediately close the website and open Twitter to see if they've picked up on the news about Josie Bishop. Out of habit, I twirl the drumstick as I scroll through the posts about Josephine Bishop.

Based on what I see, people are excited about a woman being chosen, but nobody believes the Wright/Bishop ticket will win.

Including me.

4

FIONA

MY FAMILY and I step out of the church building and submit to the veracious throng of fans and press waiting outside.

I instinctively look to my father. He's smiling brightly. He and I thrive off the people's excitement and energy. Their hope for a better tomorrow fuels my vision of seeing my father stroll into the White House as its next occupant.

I don't crave the attention or the grander life living in the White House could offer, but I want the opportunity for him more than his supporters do... or even my mother, ever could.

I've become accustomed to the uproar. The claps. The cheers. The God Bless You's. We now hear them everywhere we go and with every event, I grow more comfortable to the attention and noise.

In the previous few months, I've learned how to extend my focus from a singular sound or voice to the vast harmony they create when they combine. The simple technique makes it more musical than a fevered fandom studying each outfit I wear and judging every bewitching gesture I make.

Bewitching. Someone used that term in a blog post last week. It was a new label to me and although they meant it as a compliment; the statement confirms that my life has changed and my every move and clothing or accessory choice are being scrutinized.

Even with the bright sunlight overhead, the strobes from the cameras flashing is blinding. My parents and I are here for everyone to see, while the people hide the faces behind cell phones raised high to capture the moment in a photo, on video, or a live feed. They rarely lower their phones long enough for me to get a glimpse of their humanity.

Millions around the world are witnessing our simple moment of leaving the church, when in reality, less than fifty people are here in person.

It's the power of social media and the Internet and how we've achieved twelve percent in the polls.

All I see are phones and camera lenses, which makes it impersonal, which is why I appreciate it when we speak directly to the people, although they often get too close.

As gracefully as possible, I descend the stairs, stand on the sidewalk between my parents, and wave to the crowd.

My stylist spent hours selecting my dress, and we practiced our walk down the steep steps inside our home frequently. We leave nothing to chance.

"Fiona!"

I turn my face toward one girl screeching my name and wave.

I look to my father and wait to follow his lead.

He glances at his Secret Service agent, Miles, who nods. It's a silent signal confirming that the advance team has searched the sector and people, and we're free to approach the crowd.

When my father first became the Vice President, Jack obsessively watched documentaries about former presidents and vice presidents, so I've seen video evidence that crowds are not always controlled. Presidents John F. Kennedy and Ronald Reagan are proof that security often isn't enough.

In this strange new world, the security team even plans a trip to a church service far in advance. Dozens of people work to make sure the outing is safe, but I still get anxious when we are in such public forums.

But my love for the people is outweighing the fear.

I follow two steps behind my parents as they walk across the street.

"Is it true that Josephine Bishop is your running mate?" a reporter shouts as another asks the same question differently. "Can you confirm Josephine Bishop's selection as your running mate?"

My father greets our audience. "Good morning, everyone! What a gorgeous Sunday."

"About Josephine Bi-"

"It's Sunday. Let's save the business for tomorrow. We all need a break, don't we?"

The reporters groan at his response, but my father maintains his composure.

He was born to be in the spotlight and always looks so natural and relaxed. They don't recognize that he practiced the greeting in the car on the way to service. He had a different tone or emphasis each time he said the phrase until he found just the right one.

I enjoy watching him at work and learn more about public relations from watching him than I ever could in school.

"Where's Jack?" a DC reporter who has been following us on the trail, asks over the roar of questions from the other journalists.

I watch my father out of the corner of my eye. He throws his head back in a laugh before playfully shaking his head and again making eye contact with the journalist. "With all that's happening in the world, that's what you want to know?"

I sense jealousy in his response. It's a new emotion that's become clear since Jack started garnering so much attention. Without even being present, Jack is showing my father up again, and his reaction is too obvious. Hopefully, one of his staffers will gently remind him to contain his reactions.

"Feeling under the weather," my father answers, salvaging the moment. "And no, I cannot confirm I have asked Josephine Bishop…" he's pivoting like a pro, although I find it interesting that he would rather discuss her than his son.

"Fiona! Fiona!"

There are several young women yelling my name, but it won't be possible to speak to each one, so I focus in on a girl who, like me, looks to be in her mid-teens. She has her arms raised and hops up and down to secure my attention. Unlike the others who dressed for show, this girl is wearing a simple t-shirt, a pair of shorts, and flip-flops. She's an all-American girl and our contrast in appearance will make for a spectacular photo op.

As my father continues to discuss Josephine, I glance at my security detail, Lana. She has pulled her brunette hair into a tight bun at the back of her long neck. She's so light of frame. I wonder if she can overpower someone should the need ever arise. But she's always high on alert. And I'm safer under her care.

Because of her sunglasses, I can't see her eyes, but she nods, giving me the go-ahead to approach the crowd. I grip my clutch in my hands and parade myself in front of the cameras as I make my way toward the girl.

The clutch houses my phone and lipstick but is otherwise empty. I carry the purse more to give me something to grip and aid me in containing my hand gestures than to carry my belongings. Flailing hands never look good on video.

"Fiona! Fiona, over here," a photographer, shouts.

As I step toward the girl and her equally casually dressed friends, I turn my head ever-so-slightly while the photographer shouting my name takes his photograph.

"Here! Here!"

With each step, I adjust the tilt or turn of my head as the paparazzi and journalists snap their photographs.

The girl continues to bounce on her toes, causing her face to be a blur. "Can we get a selfie?"

Like always, I oblige. I have an inability to say 'no' to anyone and the more I practice, the less off-the-cuff discussions make me nervous. Taking more after my father than mother, I enjoy the people as long as they're friendly and non-combative.

My father and I catch each other's eye. He nods, showing his approval of my interaction, and with my hands on my clutch in front of me, I step up to the girls. "Thanks so much for coming out." I shake their hands with a gentle grip, although coming into physical contact with strangers is my least favorite part. As it is, I've never been a person who thrived on physical touch, so having so many strangers wanting to touch me causes me to hide away as soon as I get a moment alone. "It's always so amazing to see people who care so much for our country," I tell them.

"Who are you wearing?" a girl asks.

"Michael Kors."

If I were at school with my peers, I could go on for hours about his latest line. I want every item.

"You wear him a lot!" she says, with an exited nod.

I confirm her assertion with a nod. Amazing that people

remember those types of details. "I can't help myself. I love everything he makes."

"I loved it when you wore that polka-dot A-line dress for the fundraiser in Baltimore."

"Oh, yes. That dress was fabulous. One of my favorites." In actuality, I don't recall which dress the girl is referring to, but it never serves the campaign to correct or question someone over something so trivial.

The girl further begs for my attention and thrusts her phone towards me.

Having done it hundreds of times before, I turn my back to the girls, bend at the knees, and smile wide.

It's a smile I've practiced thousands of times in the mirror and in front of my poise coach. I intend to express friendliness without appearing over thought or counterfeit. It also delivers a consistent image to magazines or social media.

The girl snaps the photo. And another. And another. "One more."

My knees tremble from my continual squatting on heels in grass, but my father shows no signs of finishing with reporters and calling me away, so I stand firm and stare at the camera lens until the girl finally lowers the phone and badgers me to honor one more request. "Can I have a hug? Pretty please."

"Sure." Again, I grasp onto my clutch a little tighter.

The girls each take turns hugging me. One even runs her hand over my curls. "Your hair is fabulous."

I have no concept why people feel they have the right to pet me as if I were a puppy. For some, it appears that being a public figure means that you become their property. They don't understand how invasive all the touching can be.

"Thank you, although I can't receive any credit for that. It must be genetic." I've always wondered if my hair is hereditary, but without knowing who my birth parents are, I'll never discover if my fashion sense — or kinky curls, run in the family.

Out of the corner of my eye, I watch a staffer pull my mother aside and whisper in her ear.

Her lips purse; the sides of her eyes tighten. She glares my direction but keeps the audience loving smile on her face and continues to nod and wave as she listens to whatever news he is passing on.

My heart stops beating and only shutters back to life when my mother cuts her eyes elsewhere. I'm relieved to know that whatever it was the staffer told her, didn't involve me.

With a twist in my wedge shoes, I turn back to the girls. "We appreciate the support."

"Thanks for coming, everyone!" My father's vocal appreciation is a cue to finish up with the crowd and head for the SUV. A signal I appreciate. The physical contact has left me more than ready to escape people's attention for a few hours.

"It was so great to meet you." I wave one more time to the group of girls and walk to join my parents.

My mother kisses my father on the cheek, wipes away the lipstick she left behind, and ever the dutiful wife, places her hand around his waist and snuggles close. "We better be going."

She directs the words at the media, but I know that my mother is gazing at her husband with as much adoration as she can muster, and it likely has to be drug all the way from her toes to her heart.

Not that she doesn't love my father, because she does. But duty often outweighs romance or family time, so their bond has become more work-related than personal.

All of our bonds have, but it comes with the territory.

"Jack is waiting for us back at the house for our weekly Sunday family brunch."

My father looks at his wife and beams, revealing his polished white teeth, and then, with a choreographed head-tilt that displays his best side, looks to the crowd. "It's our favorite time of the week."

Our favorite time of the week because it's the scheduled hour in the week where we can all be present.

I watch the girls swoon at his statement. By far the most handsome of anyone else running for the presidency and youngest by at least a decade. My father winning the young female vote will be a cakewalk.

We wave our goodbyes, walk to the SUV, and duck inside as the snap of photos continues.

As soon as the door closes, a junior staffer squirts hand-sanitizer in our palms. I rub my hands together until the liquid disappears into my skin, then pull my iPhone from my clutch, hold the phone in my hand, and scroll through the Twitter feed to find out just how much damage the leak has done.

"She's trending on Twitter," I announce.

"Someone leaked it early." My father is infuriated. My gut churns. He hates when things don't go according to plan, and a leak of his choice for a running mate was not part of his plan. And could be catastrophic.

"Our people?" I ask because it wouldn't be unheard of for a staff member to leak information to an ever-hungry media.

"Of course not, Fiona," my mother purrs, brimming with sarcasm. "Nobody announces something of this magnitude on a Sunday morning."

"Cate, we didn't announce." My father's nostrils flare and his lips curl downward into a severe frown. "The press will tear her apart." He places his elbow on the window and rests his chin on his tight fist.

Whoever leaked the information, timed it perfectly. News organizations were ahead of the selection enough that the story has made it on the air of the Sunday morning political talk shows, and they printed articles – ready to be devoured by a nation just waking up on a Sunday morning or coming home from church service. "They mention her child. A daughter. Tucker-Grace Bishop."

"I hope Josie is ready for this," he says.

"Josie?" I cross one leg over the other and remove my shoes, agitated by the news. "It's Tucker-Grace you need to worry about."

5

IT's hot as literal hell.

I dip into the water to my chin and then pop back up and let Cody continue where he left off. He's nibbling on my neck, which I enjoy but wish I didn't.

We're broken up — although anyone who watches our ridiculous displays of affection from the shoreline wouldn't think so. Our friends lay scattered around shore on towels, soaking up the rays, but I can't fathom the desire to lay there and bake. It's never been my thing.

"Fiona Wright. From zero to a hero in a matter of weeks." Savannah scoffs from her spot a few feet away on her burnt orange and white striped towel. She's lying on her stomach and studying her phone as she soaks in damaging UVA rays and scans social media for the latest celebrity gossip. Some people are addicted to alcohol. Others, drugs. Some, sex. But Savannah, she's addicted to social media and celebrity gossip. If her phone's in her hand, she's getting her fix.

A Nerf football lands in the water beside us with a splash. Cody retrieves the ball, walks to more shallow water and throws the football back to the guys on shore. I watch him wade through the water. His wide, muscular back, covered in pellets of water, shimmers in the bright sun.

Cody was born and bred to be a bull rider. The red dirt from the floor of the bull riding practice facility stains his skin and flows through his veins. He loves every second, thrives on danger and attention, and bull riding cultivates both.

His body far-outshines that of our classmates. Wrangling cattle, riding bulls, and continuous aerobic training make him look much older than his seventeen years. I sympathize with the others. It's hard to compete with a guy who's an amateur bull-rider.

Compared to Cody, they look like ninth graders instead of soon to be juniors.

"I'd never even heard of her until a few weeks ago but look at her," Savannah says, as Cody returns to me. "She's stunning."

Beside her, Cassidy is fully dialed in on her own phone too. They must be looking at the same social media feed. "She was born for this. I mean, look at her. I guess that's what happens when your dad is in the running to be the leader of the free world. I wish I had her clothes. Wait, are those Jimmy Choo?"

"Tuck," Savannah says. "You better come here and look at this."

There's nothing I'd rather do less. Gossip and the choice of shoes some famous person put on their feet doesn't interest me in the slightest. I blow off her suggestion and tilt my head to the left, giving more of my neck for Cody to nuzzle.

"I'm not kidding." Savannah says, more frantic. "You really need to look at this. Your mom's trending on Twitter."

My heart shutters. Trending? On Twitter?

Why would a US senator be trending on Twitter? She's

unknown. Maybe she's dating a famous man. All other options… arrest, accident… death… It wouldn't be death. Someone would've pulled me out of church this morning to tell me.

The faster my mind races with horrible scenarios, the quicker my heart races and the more the tips of my fingers numb.

Wishing I could hide away from whatever news is about to ruin my day, and before Savannah can say another word, I dip into the water and submerge myself. Because of recent rains, the water is a little murky and my vision is limited but, to my relief, it muffles the voices cackling from shore.

I've never been a fan of noise.

My lungs burn, and my throat aches, but I don't want to resurface yet. I somehow know that as soon as I break through the surface of the water, my life is gonna change.

I plant my feet on the silt-covered lake bottom, push off and thrust through the surface of the water.

"…she's the number one topic."

I wipe the water from my face and wade to shore, but Cody stops me with a yank of my arm, pulls me close, and kisses me. Full tongue action — which I wasn't expecting or wanting. Not when I may be about to receive some of the worst news of my life.

I shove him away, walk to the girls, snatch a towel off the ground, and dry my legs off. "What did she do now?" I'm trying to act like I'm not freaking out, although I'm probably not convincing. "Is it a guy?"

"A guy? Sort of, but not how you're thinking." Savannah holds up her phone so I can read the news for myself.

Still dripping wet, I lean over at the waist, squint in the sun, and try to read the Twitter feed.

...Quaid Wright has selected freshman US Senator Josephine Bishop as his running mate...

"Wait." I've misunderstood somehow and need further inspection. I wipe my hands on the towel to dry them off and snatch the phone from Savannah's hand. "What?"

Cody places his chin on my shoulder and reads the Twitter feed. "Cool. Your mom's running for Vice President."

"Cool?" I fling the phone back to Savannah. "This is how I find out? From Twitter?" I yank a pair of cut-off blue jeans over my wet bikini bottoms.

Please don't be true. She wouldn't have kept something like this from me. It can't be true.

I start the quarter-mile walk back home. Cody's close on my heels. "Isn't this good news? Why are you mad?"

"Stay here, Cody. I'll call you later."

He halts, and I don't say another word as I walk away. There's no way he could understand the rage building in me unless he compares it to one of the bulls he tries to ride for at least eight seconds.

My mom's been acting weird the last few weeks. She hasn't called much and when we talk, she can never give me much time. She asks if anything exciting happened at church, or with Cody, and then once I give a quick download, she excuses herself and hangs up.

Even with her away from the Capitol and home for the weekend, I haven't seen her much. She's been tucked away in her home office and since I went out with Cody last night and got home late, and then got up and went to church with my aunts this morning, I haven't seen her since late yesterday afternoon.

I thought maybe it was because of a guy. She hasn't been in a serious relationship since before I was born, so it's about time she finds someone, but I've only got another two years left at home before college, so I was sort of hoping she'd wait until I was gone. Our time is limited together as it is. Adding a man to the equation would only make matters worse.

But I'd now far prefer it over this option. If the news is true, I'm not about to share her with a man. I'm about to share her with the world.

I forgot my shoes back at the other side of the lake, and my feet are burning on the hot blacktop of Lake Shore Drive, which helps me make good time. I can't tell if the water running down my back is from the lake, or if I'm sweating from the heat. And my anger.

I top the embankment and see a mass of press members lining the street by my house. My aunt Elliot's standing in the yard with a hose in her hand, spraying the lawn edge to keep them off the grass. "This is private property!"

She's still in the dress she wore to church, but she's pulled her brunette hair into a high ponytail on her head, and she's stomping across the yard in the rain boots she normally keeps on the front porch. Given that she and Sawyer always go to lunch with other church staff members after church, she's probably just arriving home and is just as shocked by this mess as I am.

Sawyer is standing a few feet back. She's scrunched up her button nose as she snickers at her sister making a fool of herself with the hose. Her freshly-cut, shoulder-length hair falls forward every time she bends over laughing.

"Elliot, how do you feel about your sister's dive into the presidential race?" a reporter, shouts.

Rather than answer, she sprays the cement near his feet, forcing him to back up. Although I'm angry, I'm with Sawyer and have to contain a laugh.

"Tucker-Grace!" My chest tightens. They've spotted me.

"Tucker-Grace!" Reporters shout my name in a terrifying wave of sound. All attention has turned to me.

Reporters run toward me, but Elliot sprays the water in the air between us, keeping them back. "Get inside," she yells. "Take Sawyer with you."

Cameras click and flash. Reporters shout ignorant questions about how I feel about my mother's announcement.

"You don't wanna know," I shout over my shoulder.

"Get inside!" Elliot screams.

Confused and angry at the avalanche of incoming news and attention, I lead Sawyer through the side yard, onto the porch, and in the back door.

I stop on the entry rug — the seal of the Great State of Texas, and wipe my feet, as I try to figure out what I'm gonna say to my mother. I've got so many questions running through my head I don't even know which one to blast her with first.

What I see and hear don't match up. There are dozens of people rummaging around, but the house is nearly silent other than Mom's muffled voice.

To the right, a group of men and women wearing business suits stand in our dining room. Their clothes are proof they're from DC; nobody dresses like that in Texas. At least not on weekends. I hate that their world is already encroaching on mine.

I zero in on Mom's voice. It's coming from the back of the house. My insides are cringing. She's talking in the fake speaking voice she uses during interviews or fundraisers. The bogus tone is like a metal knife scraping against a glass plate. It makes my skin crawl.

The front door slams, and Elliot stomps towards Sawyer and me. "She—!"

"Shh." Several people hush her, which doesn't go over

very well. Elliot eyes them with hostility and looks back at me. "She has a lot of explaining to do."

"Tell me about it."

Flanked by my aunts, I walk to the library where several, of what I can only assume are Secret Service agents due to the way they're dressed in matching dark suits and all have earbuds in their ears, are collecting around the room and whispering amongst themselves.

"The advanced team is prepping for their arrival. Sweeping the Four Seasons," one says.

"We're ghost until a formal announcement," a second adds. "No visual show of force at this point." He turns and eyes me, quickly followed by a second agent, and then, all of them.

The weight of their attention is uncomfortable, but I push the queasiness it causes aside and continue on a mission to find my mom.

A large gathering of suit-wearing individuals circles the dining room table. Paperwork, laptops, cell phones, posters, and campaign paraphernalia cover the surface.

The signs read: Wright choice for America.

So, on the nose, it's ridiculous.

"Helen, what does the schedule look like," a man asks quietly.

A woman with two pairs of eye-glasses hanging around her neck, and her grey hair in a bun, studies papers in her hand and shakes her head. "The Vice President wants her in DC, so they can try to come up with a plan. He wants to squeeze it in before his fundraiser tonight."

Tonight?

This has must have been in the works for weeks, if not months, and nobody thought to tell me. Not even my own mother.

Like a longhorn bull has stepped on my chest, my breathing gets more difficult. I pull away from the chaos of the dining room and walk towards the formal living room. My anticipation and anxiety grow exponentially when I see Mom sitting on a stool and speaking directly into a camera.

She's basically wearing a mullet. Business on top, a party on the bottom. She's wearing a crisp white dress-shirt and the jacket to her favorite red suit, but out of the view from camera, she's got on a pair of jeans and her cream-colored cowboy boots. Her dark-blonde hair is in light curls around her face, and she's wearing a full face of make-up. Even a heavy, classic red lip stain.

Yep, she planned this.

Lighting, crew, and cameras fill the room, meaning they must've brought all the equipment in after I left for church this morning. She's betrayed me more than I'd realized. She planned this to happen while I was out of the house.

"I'm honored to be in consideration," Mom's saying, "And if selected, will look forward to traveling across this great country to share a plan to bring this country back to its full glory." Mom pauses, probably listening to the interviewer's voice pipe into the earbud tucked inside her ear. She reacts to a question nobody else in the room hears, with a polite smile and a head nod. "You too, Connie. Thank you for having me."

"And we're out," the camera operator announces.

I step in to the room. My muscles are trembling, and my hands curl into fists. "What the hell? You're running for Vice President?"

6

JACK

I REFRESH the screen and the trending topics list changes. Josie Bishop is now ranked number two. Ranked number one: Tucker-Grace Bishop.

Grace?

In all the conversations I'd heard about Josie, they mentioned a Tucker, but I assumed it was a guy. The name proves otherwise.

I click on the trend link.

My breath stalls and blood rushes to my head, making my head pound more. Photos of Tucker-Grace's bikini-clad body fill the timeline, and I wouldn't be able to pull my attention away from the photos even if Tanner walked back in my room right now.

I've surprised myself. In part rebellion to being coerced into spilling campaign secrets, and partly out of sheer laziness, I didn't do any research on Josie Bishop before I leaked her name and the announcement. A simple search of the Internet would've told me more about Tucker-Grace, and this news wouldn't be a surprise. Although, I appreciate such a great shock to the system to wake me from the near coma I've been in since I Tanner woke me up.

Tucker-Grace Bishop is a blonde-headed, sixteen-year-old, All-American girl with a body destined to trend on social media, and seeing her in her swimsuit, and so obviously frustrated by the media taking her photos, does more than a cup of coffee ever could.

This should be fun.

I pick up my cell phone, open my Instagram app, and go straight to Tucker-Grace Bishop's account.

Her photos don't look choreographed or well thought out. More likely, they're moments of chance. Things and people, she wants to remember, not pictures taken to impress, like most of us do.

And none of them look like she took them in DC.

Several photos of her and a cowboy. I click on one. She mentions his name, Cody, and uses the hashtag, BullRider. I twirl the drumstick faster, and close the app.

Outside the window, SUVs roll across the drive. My parents are back from their photo op. Or what most people call "church".

My parents returning home means that I'll have to postpone my investigation into Tucker-Grace Bishop, and that's annoying. More annoying than Sunday brunch with the family — which is non-negotiable, so poking around in her life will have to wait until I can ditch them and shelter away in my room.

I walk to the window and watch everyone climb out of the car. Like snakes shedding their skin, my parents and Fiona slither out of their costumes. Dad's removing his tie, and Fiona's shoes are already off, and I can see Mom remove her earrings before she disappears under the patio.

Sunday brunch is the one meal that we eat together every

week. My parents try for more, but Sundays are a must, so I play my part and join them. At least they attempt to stay connected, so I've got to give them credit for that.

Unable to put them off any longer, I head down the stairs and watch them from the bottom step as they walk to a buffet displayed in front of the windows.

Dad stands in front of the table of food, puts his hands on his hips and takes a deep breath, reminding me more of the Brawny character from the paper towel commercials than a Vice President. "Eggs Benedict. My favorite."

"They look spectacular," Mom says.

They're eggs. Eggs my parents see every Sunday. This too, their excitement about eggs, is an act for their staffers. A staffer today could be an ex-staffer tomorrow, so it's best if they don't have ammunition against us if they leave.

With my parents here lately, everything is a production. What I don't think they realize is that everyone around them is acting too. Faking interest. Faking that they care. They're all pretending that if my dad's position suddenly fell away, they all wouldn't scatter like roaches to the next person they could leech power and connection from.

Dad turns to a junior press secretary. "Cliff, why are two of those televisions on the same channel?"

We have four TVs in the dining room. My dad had them installed so he could watch the news at all times.

Dad shakes his head. "If someone finds out that we have one station dedicated to two televisions, and they'll think I'm partial. Can you imagine what a storm that'll cause?"

"Sorry sir."

Unfortunately, Dad's right. Favoritism toward one new channel over another would have people trying to analyze his policies based on the narrative of the channel he supports. It's ridiculous.

CNN. MSNBC. Fox News. Three different channels whose coverage couldn't be more different. I didn't realize it until we had all three playing next to each other. It's like watching three different versions of a movie, and in each one the bad guy is someone different. The villains range from being President Kirkland, to Congress, to the Speaker of the House or the Senate Majority Leaders. Other times the press is pointing fingers at each other. And often, the bad guy is the voters who dare not believe all the crap the "journalists" are shoveling on their "news" channels twenty-four hours a day.

The fourth television airs CSPAN so we look more cultured.

"Look at them." Fiona stops and motions to the banners at the screens. "They don't even attempt to hide their goal of having citizens despise one another." She walks past the entryway with her plate of food.

I enter the dining room but wait for the staffers to make their plates before I make my own.

"We watched Josie's interview in the car," Dad says. "Under the circumstances, I think she handled it well. Back to its former glory was a superb touch."

"Beautiful touch," Mom confirms.

"Full. Full glory," Skip, my dad's campaign chief of staff, corrects. He's like a gnat, always hovering around. "Hamilton changed it at the last minute."

"Under your direction?" Dad asks.

Skip nods like a good dog awarded for sitting on command. "I suggested we find some wording that would sit with the people longer."

I doubt his claim. He'd take credit for the drafting of the Constitution if he thought he could get away with it, and he thought it would advance his career.

Dad turns in his seat, points his fork at Skip and smiles

wide. "That's why I hired him as my speechwriter, and you to run this campaign. Good call." He turns back to the table and takes another bite of eggs.

"On email, text or over the phone?" I ask Skip.

His eyes narrow and he adjusts his stance. "Email, text or phone what?"

I lean against the wall, still waiting on the others to finish making their plates. "How did you suggest different wording from Hamilton?"

"Email. Why?"

I shrug. "No reason."

Gotcha. I'll hack his email to confirm my suspicion that he had nothing to do with the change. Not that it matters, or I'll do anything with the information, but that amount of sucking up drives me crazy, and I just want to confirm my hunch.

Fiona stabs a chunk of cantaloupe with the tip of her fork. "A photo of her offspring in her bikini is trending on Twitter."

I now wish I hadn't leaked the news about Josie. They didn't have time to ready themselves. Tucker-Grace wasn't prepared for the ambush, and the first impression the world has on her is of an angry girl in a bikini.

Fiona throws the piece of fruit into her mouth, chews, and swallows. "Her friends call her Tuck. Can you imagine the derivatives they'll use on social media?"

"It'll be vulgar." Mom tisks.

"Josie and her daughter arrive at four," Skip continues.

I finally walk to the buffet, trying to appear casual and only moderately interested in the topic of Tucker-Grace Bishop. "I think she looks interesting."

"Interesting?" Fiona scoffs at my comment.

I pick up the one paper plate on the table and load it with eggs. I can't stand to use the china that everyone else uses because it's been around for decades, and I don't trust myself not to break it.

"... you'll have a quick greeting followed by a meeting," Skip continues. "They'll be back on the plane in a matter of hours."

I pass by the fruit and pluck two biscuits from a platter, cut them open, and slather them with butter and honey. "Like she possesses a mind of her own."

"Nobody in politics possesses a mind of their own, Jack," Fiona says.

"Nor should they," Mom adds.

"They will have to reign her in," Fiona says. "A concept she should understand since her boyfriend takes part in horse wrangling."

"He's a bull rider, Fiona, not a horse wrangler," I remind her. "You act like that's a bad thing."

"It's worse," Fiona argues. "Animal rights organizations will chew her up and spit her out completely torn to pieces."

I snatch several slices of bacon from the chafing dish. "They're from Texas. What do you expect?"

"How do you know her boyfriend is a bull rider?" she asks.

"Same way you thought he was a horse wrangler. The Internet."

"Jack, Fiona," I turn to my dad as he wipes his mouth with his cloth napkin and wrings it in his hands. "With her mother comes thirty-eight electoral votes. I don't give a damn what the girl's boyfriend does."

"Fiona, Jack." I now look to Skip, who's trying to keep us all on task. "You two will have an early supper with Tucker-Grace while your father meets with Josie."

It's the best news I've heard all morning.

"What do we call her?" Fiona asks with pure contempt on

her lips. "Tucker-Grace? Tucker? Tuck?" She choked that last option out of her throat.

"How about we just call her by her name? Tucker-Grace." I pick up one more piece of bacon and walk to the table. "Or call her thirty-eight electoral votes since that's all we truly care about."

I glance at my dad for a reaction, but he only raises an eye brow.

"We won't inform the press of this meeting," Skip continues. "But if they show up, this is a simple dinner. Getting to know the daughter of a possible running mate."

"Hair and make-up arrive at two," Robin says, frantically entering the room with the usual yellow mechanical pencil shoved behind her ear.

I take a bite of bacon. "Based on Tucker's Instagram feed, she's -"

"Jack! You didn't follow her account-" My sister's paranoia is disturbing.

"No."

Fiona ignores my denial and continues on her panicked train of thought. "If you follow her before the official announcement, it will be another scoop. It will-

"Chill. I said I didn't follow her."

Fiona rubs her forehead in annoyance. "Is she verified?"

"No." I noticed it when I studied her account. No blue check mark. Only a few hours ago she was a normal girl from Texas, that's rapidly changing.

Blue check marks are currency and whether you have one is consideration of where you land in the hierarchy at school. If we weren't out of school for the summer and Tucker-Grace went to All Saints, getting a blue check mark would send her spiraling into the upper echelon of All Saints High society.

Mom drops her silver fork to the table, leans against the back of the chair, and places her hands in her lap. "Skip."

Skip hops to it and practically prances to her side. His pandering is disgusting. "Ma'am?"

"Get the girl verified. I don't even want to think about what might show up on faux-accounts."

"Yes, Ma'am."

"Mother, is that necessary?" Fiona crosses her arms over her midriff. "That blue check-mark is valuable. It-"

"Of course, it's necessary."

Fiona sits back in her seat and sulks. It took her months to earn the blue checkmark. Tucker-Grace may get it within minutes.

Enough to get tongues wagging and make the girls who have been fighting their way to the top, furious. Including my sister.

Skip walks to an intern who, as far as I know, has no name. At least not as far as anyone in the room is concerned. Skip whispers into the unknown person's ear and then quickly returns to Dad as the staffer scurries away like a rat looking for a piece of cheese.

"Why are you defending a girl you haven't even met?" Fiona asks, still on the topic of Tucker-Grace and seemingly wanting to stay there.

My neck tightens and my fingers tense around my plastic fork. "Why are you demonizing her?"

"I'm not, but I can assure you the press will."

I toss my fork onto the table and push my paper plate away. "Then why don't you leave it alone and let them have at it. She doesn't need you piling on."

"You're acting like you two know each other or something."

"Or…" I shrug. "I don't know, maybe I'm a decent person."

Fiona chuckles at the prospect. "Nice try."

Dad throws his napkin down on to the table, taking command of the conversation. "Children are off limits. The press won't touch Tucker."

Press may not, but bloggers and trolls will. Fiona and I know that full well. The press tries to be cordial and give us our space. Casual "journalists", social-media agitators and bloggers go for the jugular.

"Tucker-Grace," Mom corrects.

"The name's a mouthful." Dad's dissatisfaction is clear and if he has his way, he'll force Tucker-Grace to change her name from one she's used for sixteen years to one with fewer syllables.

"It's Southern," I tell him. "You'd know that if you paid any attention to a state that isn't blue."

"I give my attention to all states, Jack. You remember that." Dad glares at me with a look that would send chills down any staffer's spine but doesn't affect me the way he hopes. I'm so accustomed to the glares; they don't phase me.

I pick up a slice of bacon. "Duly noted." I shove the bacon in my mouth and pick up the plastic fork again.

Aside from not wanting to use the priceless plates and silverware laid out for me, the paper plate and a plastic fork are my silent middle finger to the members of the All Saints Green Planet Society. One of their members saw me drinking from a plastic water bottle and in response the group ran an ad in the school paper about how I wasn't a friend to the planet. For almost a month, I was the worst human being on the earth, until Sean Wingham dared to shoot a gun at a firing range with some cousins. The pictures made it onto Instagram, and students turned their hatred to him and kept it there for the better part of the spring semester.

After Hunter, I think it was Melody Hamm. According to some, she showed too much side boob in her prom dress and caused a near hysteria-inducing battle between the various sides of women's rights issues. That kept everyone busy and preoccupied until school ended for the summer.

"Anyway." I retrieve my plate so I can dive into my eggs before they get cold. "I just think we should give the girl a chance before we assume she can't handle all of this."

"Nobody can handle all of this." Fiona clamps her mouth shut and keeps her eyes on her plate. "It's just a lot. That's all."

Fiona does well at hiding the pressure. Occasionally the facade cracks, but rarely in front of anyone but me.

"Especially for a girl from Texas." My observation is meant to cover hers.

It must work. Dad moves right on and doesn't press her on her comment. "It'll be our job to help with the transition. Which is why I asked her to bring her daughter and the three of you will go to dinner. While I help Josie prepare, I will need you two to do the same with Tucker."

"Tucker-Grace." I shove a fork full of eggs into my mouth and pretend not to notice another hostile glare from Dad.

Once brunch is over and the staffers have fully informed Fiona and me about our plans for the day, and Dad dismissed us, Fiona and I walk up the stairs to our rooms.

"I don't think you should be so hard on her," I tell her. "I mean, I know you don't like her but-"

"I never said I didn't like her."

Shocked by her denial, I halt, turn and look down the stairs towards the dining room we just left and where she oozed disdain. "All of that down there was not you disliking her?"

"No. That was me realizing that we're about to be front and center, and that girl isn't prepared for that kind of attention."

"Like you said, who is? They threw us into this the same way they did her."

"No. We've been preparing for this for seven and a half years."

I lean against the stair railing and search her face, hoping to see some sign of humanity. That she hasn't completely succumbed to this world to the point that she has no compassion for what Tucker-Grace is being thrown into. Not knowing I'm the one that threw her into it. "You can't believe that crap."

"Dad said-"

"Yeah, well, Dad says… and does a lot of things. And he made this decision without asking our opinion or giving a heads up."

Fiona swivels, about to head into her room, but I tug on her elbow. "Come on, Fie-. Can't you at least admit that you were a little blindsided by the timing of this too?"

She nods reluctantly. "Maybe so. But you can't trust anyone." She leans to me and stares me right in the eyes. "Not even family."

With a spin she perfected in years of dance class, Fiona enters her room and slams the door behind her.

I stare at the closed door for several seconds unable to move out of fear that she's on to me.

No, she can't be. I'm just being paranoid.

I walk up to the third floor, into my room, and close and lock the door before I head back to my computer and enter the chat room.

I sit staring at the blinking cursor, doubting whether I should continue to leak information. At the least, Fiona's flailing with doubt about who in our inner-circle we can trust and if I continue on, I'll become one person she can't.

If I haven't already crossed that line.

But I have to keep telling them what I know. If she thinks life is uncertain now, it will only get worse if I don't continue disclosing information. And now, with another innocent girl being dragged into the madness, I'm more determined to keep feeding material into the invisible world of the dark web.

I stare at my drums and then give in to the pressure, start a new message and type: Photo op. Dinner at Sushiniko. 4:30pm.

WITH THE INTERVIEW OVER, the noise in the house gets louder and louder, and even the thought my mother invited everyone into our home under these circumstances, its's an invasion, and I'm more pissed than ever.

The camera crew dismantles their equipment as a second television news group moves in.

I fold my arms across my stomach. Water drips down my back. "You can't be serious."

Mom looks back at me with wide, guilty eyes like a kid who just got caught with their hand in the candy jar. It's a look I rarely, if ever, have seen from her. At least directed at me. She tells me everything.

Or used to.

"Seems like your big plans for the future have clouded your vision and sensitivity scale leading you to not discuss some pretty big news with your only child."

A smile slips off Mom's face as she slides off the stool. "I was going to tell you."

It wounds me, that my mother doesn't have a better explanation. I hoped for some cataclysmic event that prevented her from discussing her plans, but to just forget or choose not to share the news?

It's cruel.

"You would tell me before or after you toured the country and shared your plan with the American people?"

Mom throws her hands into the air in surrender and walks out of the room.

"Or hordes of reporters camped out on our property?" Elliot adds as we follow Mom through the first floor of the house. If she's trying to evade our questions, she's gonna fail. She owes me… us, an explanation.

Some people who I know as senate staffers and others who I assume are a part of the campaign move around our house in full business mode. None of them seem the least bit concerned that my life just imploded.

The campaign must've set up computers around the house so they could each watch the news from their work space because I could swear I've passed at least four and with everyone we pass, the more reality sinks in because my mom is the leading story on every single website.

I stop and look at footage of her during her Senate campaign. "Wow, it's all happening in real time. I'm finding out my mother is running for Vice President the same time the rest of the world is."

"They weren't going to announce for a few weeks, but the decision somehow leaked early." She tosses the words over her shoulder at us like she's tossing salt while making Thanksgiving dinner. Like it's trivial. A game.

I don't even know this woman. Four years ago, my mother would've never acted so cavalier.

I push ahead of Mom and turn to face her, forcing her to come to a stop and make eye contact. "A decision to leak when the opportunity wasn't discussed?"

She averts her eyes and looks to a television. She can't even make herself look at me. She knows she's wrong. "I discussed it," she mutters.

I step towards her. "Not with me."

"Or us," Elliott adds.

Mom's personal assistant, Beth, approaches out of nowhere. She could've been with us the entire time, but I'm so blinded by fury I didn't notice. "Skip approved the CNN interview. You go live in ten. They're setting up now."

Beth's hair is more teased than usual. She lives by the creed, "the bigger the hair, the closer to God" and I get it, but the girl needs too tame it down a little. And get out of my face.

"Same talking points?" Mom asks, back on the sidetrack and throwing me over the edge.

"You know nothing but would be honored..."

"Beth, could I please have ten seconds with my mother?" I have to force the words out of a tense jaw and gritting teeth.

A little taken back by the hostility in my question, Beth slinks away while applying more lip gloss.

I turn to Elliot and Sawyer and wait for them to catch a clue. Finally, they register that my stare is a silent demand for them to leave me alone with my mother, and, like Beth, exit the room. But minus the lip gloss.

When I return my attention back to Mom, she's finally making eye contact.

"And I asked how something leaked because I know that you would never agree to something as monumental as running for Vice President of the United States without talking to me about it first."

'I know, I-"

"And I asked because over my entire life you've instilled

in me the fact, we're a team, and we make major life decisions together."

"Tuck, I-"

A voice on the computer screen closest to us, ends our conversation. I stop and listen. "Vice President Wright would select US Senator Josephine Bishop because of her strong economic record, stance on immigration, oil and natural gas PAC support, and an obvious appeal to female voters. A single mother of one, Bishop quickly rose through political ranks winning the Senate seat just four years ago after a successful career in the military…"

They show photos of my mother throughout her career as they continue to talk about the numerous reasons the Vice President would select her.

"… Josephine's daughter, Tucker-Grace, is from small-town Texas and may not be prepared for life in DC."

A split screen reveals both Fiona and me. Fiona's exiting church in a perfectly styled dress and looking like she just walked out of a Glamour magazine shoot, and I'm walking up to my house in a barely-there bikini top and butt-cheek revealing cut-off shorts like I've just left a shift at Hooters.

It's humiliating.

Mom winces at the final sentence, and shakes her head, maybe finally feeling some remorse.

Disgusted by all of it, I race up the steps and yell over my shoulder. "And you wouldn't do something that might pull me out of my school and take me away from Cody and my friends all so you can make your latest power grab."

"Power grab?" She shouts. "I care about the American peop-"

I stop at the top step and turn to face her, but she's still several steps away. "Spare me the stump speech. Unlike the American people, I ain't buying it."

She opens her mouth to shout again, but her face softens. "Wait, I thought you and Cody broke up. Again."

"It's complicated." I walk into my bedroom. "Always complicated."

I spin around to dive right back into our argument, but she's followed into the room by staffers. I'm smothered by their presence.

Mom's stylist, Liz, tosses a suitcase onto the bed and then disappears into my closet. It's always amazed me she's a stylist. She's only in her mid-twenties and dresses more plainly than almost anyone I've known. Her hair is always in a loose ponytail and the hair band looks like it could slip out of her thin hair with even the slightest turn of her head.

But she's good at what she does. When it comes to my mom. I don't trust her to choose anything for me.

I try to ignore the fact that Liz just inserted herself into my closet and is going through my things and focus back on Mom. "This is all out of the bad dream. Do you realize that?"

Mom walks to me and runs her hand down my arm to soothe and calm me, but it won't work. "Stella and I were talking, and -"

My agitation returns. "Who's Stella?"

"Me." Stella steps forward and holds out her hand for a polite handshake. "I'm your mother's campaign Chief of Staff."

And she's stunning. She reminds me of an actress I watched in a Netflix series with Turkish subtitles. Her eyes are a goldish-brown, and she's got her hair pulled into a loose bun on her neck. If the campaign thing doesn't work for her, she could be a model.

My phone rings. I pull it from my back pocket and see it's Cody. "Wait till he hears about this."

Stella shakes her head, reaches out and lowers my arm

before I can put the phone to my ear. "Don't discuss any of this with him."

I let the phone continue to ring. "My sometimes boyfriend can't hear about boring campaign talk?"

Stella removes her hand from my arm and clasps her hands in front of her. "We haven't vetted him."

"Vetted? He's seventeen. How much could he have done at this point?"

"You'd be surprised."

With every passing moment, this entire thing is getting more preposterous. I've almost completely transitioned from anger to amusement.

But only almost.

I hang up and shove the phone back into my rear jean-shorts pocket. "What does he have to do? Sign a confidentiality agreement in blood?"

"Only if we win." Stella smirks at me. I'm sure that if circumstances were different, I'd like her. Right now, however, she's pulling my mom further away from me.

"Stella says we need to get you some speaker training," Mom says.

Shocked, reeling, and unable to keep up with the constant interruptions, I try to focus on Mom. "What's wrong with how I talk?"

"How you talk is fine," Stella says. "But talking and speaking are two separate things. We won't ask you to speak often, but you need to be prepared for when the time comes."

Sitting on the bed, I tuck one leg under me and stare at the fishbowl. I can sort of understand how the pathetic thing must feel. It lives its entire life exposed to the outside world. How miserable. "I'd prefer not to speak at all. It's not my job."

"I don't have a spouse," Mom blurts.

And I don't have a father, but that hasn't seemed to bother her before. "Not my fault."

"You're all I've got."

"Correction, I'm all you had." A room full of staffers stare back at me. "Looks like you've got plenty now." I roll my eyes to Stella, who looks just as uninspired as me. "I took a speech class at school. Does that count for anything?"

"I'm afraid not. This is a different type of speech."

"The kind where you lie?" I ask.

"Pretty much. The campaign is sending someone to work with you." Stella's lightening her tone a little. "They'll give you sound bites, polite responses, and the like. They'll be with us on the trail."

"Us?" I lay back onto the bed and hug a pillow to my chest to control my urge to puke.

Mom shrugs, innocently. "It'll be fun."

Fun. The thought of traipsing around the country spouting rehearsed lines and soundbites doesn't sound the least bit like fun. At least not for someone who hates being in the spotlight, like me.

"Says who?" I ask.

"Whom," Stella corrects, with another smirk. Now she's just playing with me. "That's why you need a speech coach. Now, shall we go over the schedule?"

"Yes, we shall." I over-emphasized the shall, playing right back.

Helen sits down in the desk chair, puts on one of the two pairs of glasses hanging around her neck, and studies her schedule. The grey tint to her hair stands out against my elephant skin colored walls. "In forty-five minutes, we depart the regional airport. We will arrive in DC, drive to the Vice President's residence for a meeting…" Helen removes a glossy pamphlet from a folder and hands it to me. It's an information sheet about the Vice President's residence.

"Number One Observatory Circle," I mutter, as I read the title. It reminds me of a house you'd see on a beach on the East Coast somewhere. Pure white siding and green shutters. It's impressive.

Helen continues. "... where Tucker-Grace, you and the Vice Presidents children will head to Sushiniko for an early dinner..."

"Sushiniko. How very-" Helen hands me an information sheet about the restaurant. "- elite sounding." I look at the photos of the restaurant. "Oh, look at that. It is very elitist."

"... After dinner with Fiona and Jack..." As Helen says their names, she pulls stapled pieces of paper out of her notebook and hands them to me. They're information sheets about each member of the Wright family. At first glance, it's their basics. Name, brief bio, and photos.

"... you will return to the residence to pick up your mother and head back home. Simple. Unless..."

I scan the first page about Quaid Wright and flip to the next. Cate Wright. They're professional photos and look stiff, but like they're trying not to look stiff. I look back up at Helen. "Unless? What does that mean?"

"Unless the Vice President decides he'd like you at his fundraiser, this evening at which point you will head to the Four Seasons..." Helen pulls out a Four Seasons brochure and hands it over. I add it to my stack of study material. "... change clothes and head downstairs to the George Washington Terrace for the private reception. After the fundraiser..."

Helen hands me another stack of papers. They're a list of names and the dollar amounts of their donations in the last election. "I'm supposed to be on summer vacation. Homework doesn't seem fair."

"You will stay the night at the Four Seasons and return to Wheaton early tomorrow morning while the rest of DC is sound asleep or too hungover to notice your departure."

I'm a wake up late, eat cereal in my pajamas sort of girl. Waking up at the crack of dawn to jump on a plane is a waste, and I haven't kept up with all the stuff spewing out of Helen's mouth. "I didn't catch all of that. When's the Four Seasons part?"

Helen hands me another sheet of paper.

"Oh, look at that. A print version of the schedule. Lovely." I can't hide my sarcasm or disdain for the upcoming ordeal.

I look over Fiona's bio.

"Fiona's adopted. That's pretty cool." I figure the Wright's can't be half-bad if they're willing to adopt a child. Especially one who appears to be biracial, which I think is awesome but prejudiced jerks around the country, won't.

Liz exits the closet carrying folded clothes and places them in the suitcase.

Frustrated, I turn to her. "I'll pack my own clothes."

She shakes her head. "I've got it under control."

"But I can do it."

"I'm packing one outfit for each portion of your trip. The flight to DC. The meet and greet and dinner. The fundraiser, should you attend, pajamas, and a final outfit for travel home."

I groan. "Five outfits? For less than 24 hours? That's ridiculous."

Liz nods as she makes room in the suitcase for more items.

"Who in the world would ever need five outfits for

twenty-four hours?" I look to Mom. "If this continues, you're gonna need to increase my allowance. I'll need a bigger clothing budget."

"The campaign will help with that," Liz tells me. "Do you own a business suit?"

I nearly recoil at the suggestions. "A suit? No, and I never will."

Flipping the information sheet, my eyes fall on Jack Wright. His blond hair is perfect. His complexion is perfect. His blue eyes, freaking perfect. And the dimples. Good lord, it's like they sculpted the perfect image of an All-American boy. "Wow." I toss the sheets of paper onto the bed and sigh. "He looks like a scandal waiting to happen."

I'm reaching a boiling point and fear that if people don't give me some space and time to think, I'm gonna explode.

When Liz adds another item to the suitcase, I reach my maximum frustration level and can't take another second. I stand, remove everything from my suitcase, and with an arm full of clothes, turn to everyone in the room. "No offense, but I'll pack my own clothes."

Liz steps forward. "But we should all have a conversation before you-"

"Yeah well," I glance at Mom. "There are a lotta things we should've had a conversation about." I step into my closet and dump the perfectly folded clothes onto the ground in a heap. "But that's no longer how we roll around here, and I guess we'll all have to get over it."

Attempting to drown out the conversation now bubbling around in my room, I slide hangers across the closet bar and inspect my clothes as I try to figure out what in the world you wear when you're about to meet the man who's a heartbeat away from the presidency.

I don't have that sort of outfit for that kind of event, so

rather than be uncomfortable all day, I'm gonna have to pick something imperfect — and maybe not even appropriate. It'll have to be enough. And if I'm not enough, the American people are better off figuring that out now, because enough is all that I can manage.

8

FIONA

JOSEPHINE AND TUCKER-GRACE were ten minutes late, and now we've been standing in this unimaginable heat for the better part of two minutes waiting for them to climb out of the SUV so we can formally greet them and welcome them to our home.

I lower my head to wipe my brow and use the cover of my hand to look to Jack. "What's taking them so long?" I whisper.

"Would you want to face us?" Jack hardly moves his lips. He'd make any ventriloquist proud.

"Point taken."

I lower my hand and raise my eyes as the door to the vehicle finally opens. Josephine steps outside with a bright smile.

She almost looks too young for such an important position, and I imagine that one of the first things our stylists will do is make her appear older and worldlier. She looks as excited, yet nervous, as a girl about to go on her first date. They will change that too. Her excitement needs to play with our audience as more of a passion for the people and an exuberance about the opportunity that lies ahead, rather than a woman who is easily excitable. Obvious fluctuation of her mood and emotions will make people fear her ability to make lucid, practical decisions.

If she were a man, however, people would appreciate that he was in touch with his emotional side.

Josephine shakes my parents' hands as Tucker-Grace exits the vehicle. It offers a first glance at a cleaned-up and beautified version of Tucker-Grace.

I can see her knees. They stand out between her suede boots, which hit her just below the kneecap and her thigh-length dress. She must not have a stylist.

It's a pity.

As I shake Josephine's hand, I glance at my mother out of the corner of my eye, and with one singular glimpse of Tucker-Grace's outfit, her lips tighten. I smile larger to cover what I'm sure is mortification on my mother's part. To her, Tucker-Grace's sense of autonomy might mean she's untamable, and that is a political concern.

To my left, Jack shakes Josephine's hand, then takes a small step toward Tucker-Grace and looks her up and down as he runs a hand over his hair. He thinks he's being sly, but his interest could not be more obvious. At least not to me.

"This is all a little awkward," my father admits. "Am I right?"

Tucker-Grace smiles and relaxes slightly. "Completely."

"They've told me that this was a surprise to you, Tucker."

I cringe internally. He's chosen to shorten her name for his own convenience, and I wonder how she feels about the change.

"Quite." Tucker-Grace doesn't correct him, which shows she has some tact.

He places a hand on her shoulder and looks down on her with a sympathetic smile. He's being more fatherly than political. "I'm sorry about that. Sideswiping you was not our intention, but someone leaked the news before we were certain."

She looks to her mother; her face revealing relief. "So, you aren't the official pick, then?"

"Oh no, she is," my father tells her. "But things like that aren't officially determined so soon."

Tucker-Grace's face falls, her gloom is clear and the awkwardness that moments ago lifted away has returned like a heavy fog. I wish they could re-enter the vehicle, and we could start this entire moment again. It would be best for all involved.

"Welcome to the Vice President's residence, Tucker-Grace," my mother welcomes warmly and returning Tucker-Grace her entire name.

"When we get back from dinner, we could give you a tour, if you'd like," I offer. "It's larger than you might think from only seeing the outside. It's over nine thousand square feet."

"But still cozy," my mother adds as if I mischaracterized the home.

"Sure. I'd appreciate that." She eyes the residence. "Cozy, huh? Not a word I would use to describe it."

My body tenses at Tucker-Grace's correction. It's unnecessary and perhaps she isn't as tactful as I initially believed. She could have simply let the word slide rather than making it an issue. It seems she likes to have the last word.

"I like it better than the White House, though. At least it looks more personal. Like a refuge instead of a showpiece for the world to see." Tucker-Grace grimaces. "And I'm rambling. Which I do. A lot, especially when I'm nervous, and I've never been more nervous that I know of. See? Rambling."

My father appears impressed and entertained by her, which I find shocking. He's rolling back on his heels and snickering.

Snickering. The man rarely, if ever, snickers—although I often elicit a chuckle out of him.

Tucker-Grace turns and eyes the grounds.

"Come January 20th, this could be your new home," my father tells her, ending her survey of the estate.

And if it doesn't become Tucker-Grace's home in January, we'll be looking for a new residence, and it won't be the White House.

She looks back at him and swallows hard. "One can hope."

Tucker-Grace isn't a good liar which isn't a good sign for someone about to be on the campaign trail, and my case for concern is mounting with evidence.

My mother reaches over and lightly grips Tucker-Grace's elbow. "You will love it. I know my children do."

Tucker-Grace shifts her focus to Jack and me, and I force a quick smile.

"I love it," I tell her, confirming my mother's declaration.

Jack shrugs and smirks. "I can't lie, it is great. And the staff will cook you whatever you want, so there's that."

They share a smile. I don't know about her, but Jack's in a flirtatious manner, and his eyes are solely focused on hers.

This may be the first moment that I'm genuinely concerned for her. I would like to call a time-out for the moment, pull her aside and warn her to keep a safe distance from my brother. He's charming and never lacks for female attention, but he lures young women in and uses his charisma as a weapon. Just as all true politicians do.

I fear that Tucker-Grace is in danger of falling into his trap, and if she does, the entire campaign will suffer from the fallout.

9
_____

THE SOUND of tires on the pavement draws everyone's attention away from my idiocy and to several vehicles pulling up the drive.

Even someone as dense as me can tell that it's the President. His limousine is the third in line and is so large, it's hard to ignore. The weirdness factor of this entire day just increased exponentially.

"I was not ready for this," I mutter to Mom.

Her eyes are wide. She shakes her head and shrugs at me and then looks to the Vice President. "I didn't realize the president was joining us." Mom's easy-confidence seems to have transformed into terror, which only makes me more nauseous.

"Neither did I," the Vice President grumbles.

I want to somehow hide behind my mother but settle for tugging on my dress to make it cover my knees. It's a useless endeavor, and I'm gutted.

Mortified, I look to Fiona who tells me, "You look great. Don't let him intimidate you. He's human, just like the rest of us."

"That's debatable," Jack grumbles.

I glance at him. He looks down at me from the step above and winks in a "you've got this" sorta way, which I appreciate but doubt.

My mother, the Wrights and I stand there surrounded by staffers and watch the President of the United States, John Kirkland, emerge with a broad Cheshire cat grin.

I swallow hard. Seeing him live and in person gives me the creeps. Someone caked his face in makeup, and he seems to have more hairspray in his hair than I've worn in a month. Combined.

The Vice President places his hands on my elbows and gently moves me aside so he can approach the latest guest. The motion leaves me standing between Fiona and Jack, so I seize the opportunity and squeeze between them, so I'm standing slightly behind.

They're smart, these two. And apparently mind-readers, because they each move towards each other, nearly hiding me completely. I'm grateful for the camouflage.

"Hello, Sir," the Vice President welcomes. "We-"

"I heard a rumor you two were meeting today," the President says, cutting the Vice President off. "I left my event a little early and came right over."

I'm not politically savvy, but I have survived two years of high school, and it's really not much different from when the prom queen makes sure that the prom court doesn't get the same attention she does. They don't ride on the same float in the parade or stand together on stage. The runners up are separate and are lesser in importance — and treated that way.

There's a hostile glance between the President and Vice President and if the press were here to witness it, the nation would realize there is no love lost between them. I'm even surprised. I always assumed Presidents and Vice Presidents had to work well together.

Seems like I assumed a lot of stuff wrong and I flat out don't have a clue what my mother's just gotten us into.

"Thought I'd join." The President winks, then goes quiet, attempting to intimidate his Vice President without so much as a word. Vice President Wright needs to get a backbone and send him on his way.

Quaid Wright stands firm for several seconds but then melts under the pressure, which bruises my heart some.

The Vice President moves aside. The President gives Mrs. Wright the Hollywood double kiss and then politely shakes Fiona's hand.

"Jack." The President walks to Jack, holds his hands behind his back and looks him up and down. "I wasn't sure you would be here."

"Where else would I be? Sir." Jack added that 'Sir' on there to cover up the disdain that almost dripped out of his mouth like spit. It's obvious he can't stand the man and just seconds after meeting the President, I can't blame him. The guy's an ass.

The President chuckles and then slaps Jack on the shoulder. "I've heard you get around town."

I glance at the Vice President wondering if he's gonna step up and stop the President from his obvious harassment of Jack. He's belittling him in some sick sort of sarcasm. It's so twisted that I'm wondering if this whole thing is a joke they're playing on us to see if we can handle the wildly weird world of politics on a global scale.

"I've heard the same about you," Jack says.

I swallow hard. *Please don't look my way.* There's no way I can hide my shock at their interaction. I'm not a good actress.

The President's smile turns to a scowl. My heart races. I'm standing here watching the most powerful man in the world stare down a seventeen-year-old kid who he sees as some sort of competition.

It's insanity, and I'm lightheaded.

The President turns to my mother and smiles. He just changed his expression in the blink of an eye, and I'm further creeped out.

I steal a glimpse of Jack in time to see him glance over his shoulder at me in return. Again, he smirks and shrugs like it's all a game and he's loving every second.

His lack of concern eases my anxiety some.

"So, you're the famous Josephine Bishop," the President says.

I look away from Jack. My body flinches as the President reaches his hand out for Mom to shake. I want to bust through the sister and brother duo and yank my mom's arm back, so she won't touch him.

But she does. "I am."

The President shakes her hand with a single, firm pump.

"What a wonderful surprise to see you on the news this morning…"

I tune the President out and focus on the brother and sister in front of me.

They have perfect posture, which I find annoying.

Fiona is regal. Or like she belongs in front of Buckingham Palace instead of One Observatory Circle. With her arms draped in front of her and hands clasped in front of her black tuxedo slacks, she is so in command of herself that I can only assume all attention turns to her when she enters a room. It's a relief. I'll be able to stay in the background because she'll draw all the attention to herself.

She's calm, collected, and elegant. Everything I'm not.

Next to Fiona, her brother is wearing gray dress slacks with a navy blue polo shirt. It's a little spiffy for a summer day, and would never pass in Wheaton, but I can't deny that Jack is as perfect looking as his sister. Cute as he is, though, he isn't my type. I prefer a guy in blue jeans and cowboy boots.

The Vice President is a handsome man who obviously works out to keep his appearances up. His black hair looks damp, but is slicked back with a light film of gel. There's a slight tint to his skin which makes since. I read that his grandfather was half Japanese. Beside him, his wife is smiling, revealing deep dimples. Her brunette hair is perfectly styled to look like she's got natural beachy waves.

I swallow hard for the umpteenth time and force myself to step between the duo so I can shake the man's hand, but he ignores my approach and walks towards the house. "Shall we take this inside?"

I hide my hand behind my back, embarrassed.

Jack places his hand on my shoulder and leans toward me. "You're better off," he whispers. When he steps away, his cologne still lingers in a mist around me.

My initial reaction to seeing Jack's information sheet may be correct. He may be a scandal waiting to happen, but he also seems to try to lessen the oddity of the moment, and give me some peace of mind, which I appreciate. He's not as bad as I'd assumed.

The man that was standing behind and just to the right of the President is looking me up and down, which is unsettling. He looks more than a handful of years older than me and has beady eyes that make him look like he doesn't have a soul.

The bowtie wearing, ogling staffer must notice that I see him eyeing me because he steps towards me.

Jack steps forward and again places me behind him and his sister.

"Sheldon Maxwell," the man says. "White House staffer."

"White House staffer? That's a generic title," Mom says.

"He has a generic job," the President tells her, over his shoulder.

"The kids were just about to leave," the Vice President announces, much to my relief. He signals something to a staffer.

"Then I'll meet you inside." The President pushes past us, walks under the covered passageway to the front door, and disappears inside with Sheldon, leaving the rest of us standing there.

"Okay, well... that was weird," I admit out loud.

The Vice President smiles over at me. "I couldn't agree more."

A black SUV pulls up.

"You kids get out of here and let us deal with the President," he says.

As soon as the door opens, I take the Vice President up on his offer and practically hurl myself inside, over the middle seat and into the back row and as far from the President and his staffer as I can get.

Fiona climbs into the second row in front of me. Jack hurdles her row and joins me in the back, which I find odd, but when he turns and focuses out the back window, I realize he wants to keep watch as the vehicle pulls past the gate and onto the road.

I've just met the President of the Freaking United States of America, and it's not even an encounter that left me inspired or in awe.

Instead, meeting the most powerful man in the world has

left me sick to my stomach, and I want nothing more than to go back to Wheaton and wipe the entire experience out of my memory.

10

JACK

I LOOK out the back window and watch to see if any of the President's henchmen will follow us to dinner.

We just witnessed a man attempting a power play, but more than anything, it left everyone confused.

Everyone but me, maybe. I don't think the president enjoyed being sideswiped, and he showed up to make it known. And he knew to show up because I leaked him the details about the meeting.

When I sent the information through the dark web, I didn't expect it to go down like that. I figured I was tipping him off to something, so he'd have more knowledge of what my dad was up to. I didn't imagine that he'd show up in our driveway and make his displeasure known.

Seeing him show up made me sick to my stomach.

I don't see any vehicles following, but he knows where we're going and will probably have a pair of eyes or two there to watch, which means I can relax for a few minutes but need to be ready to be on the look-out once we arrive at the restaurant.

My mom suggested that the three of us eat at home on

the back patio so we could have some privacy, but Skip advised that we eat in public so the campaign could confirm the allegation of Josie's selection without coming right out to say it.

We're political pawns and even though it didn't settle well with me at first, it's better than being at home right now with the President trying to usurp his power.

So, here we are heading out together and throwing Tucker-Grace to the wolves. After just meeting the vicious alpha of the wolf pack.

I steal a look at her. She's wringing her hands in her lap causing the bracelets hanging around her wrists to jingle. With each clink of the bracelets, my guilt piles up for involving her in all of this and with no thought of how Josie's daughter would be affected.

I wish I could tell her it will all work out and be all right, but I can't tell her that. I don't know that it will be.

"So... Is that normal? For the President to come to meetings like this?" Tucker-Grace asks, finally sitting back into her seat.

"No." I turn back around and face the front.

"Including today," I say, holding a fist in front of my face. "I can count on one finger..." I raise one finger... the middle. "The number of times that man has been to the house."

Fiona reaches over the seat back and slaps my hand. I lower the offensive digit and laugh.

"Were you as surprised by all of this as I was?" Tucker-Grace asks. "I mean, the announcement."

"Surprised by his selection? No," Fiona tells her. "Surprised by the timing? Absolutely. Normally, the Vice-Presidential selection isn't announced until a few days before the party conventions."

"Why's that?" Tucker-Grace asks.

"It's a momentum thing," Fiona says. "And it gives the press less time to uncover-"

"Skeletons in the closet?" Tucker-Grace swallows hard and rests her forehead on the window. "They're gonna rip her to shreds, aren't they?"

Bothered by her sudden concern, I lean forward, so I can get a better look at her. "Not if the campaign can help it."

She looks over her shoulder and smiles weakly at me. There's an innocence in her eyes I don't normally see in people I hang out with. She's wilting under the weight of the upcoming spotlight. Most people in DC would thrive on it.

I reach out to touch her arm but think better of it and put my hand in my lap. "We'll launch and adjust. This may not have happened the way the campaign would have wanted it, but my dad's campaign staff are the best in the business. They'll figure out a way to spin this to our favor." I eye her hands, and the jingling of the bracelets around her wrists has quieted. Her hands are more still. "We'll be all right. I promise."

Her eyes are green, and her nose splattered in freckles. Again, she smiles at me, and some freckles disappear when her nose scrunches.

"I'm impressed with his selection."

My body tenses momentarily at the sound of Fiona's voice. I had almost forgotten she was in the car with us. I force myself to look away from the gold flecks in Tucker-Grace's eyes and focus on my sister, as she lays her arm on the back of the seat and relaxes. With nobody to watch us, she can breathe a little easier.

We all can.

I compare her bare fingers and the small watch on her wrist to Tucker-Grace's whose are covered in rings and bracelets.

It's like something out of central casting when we're looking for people to be in Dad's election commercials and trying to show that he appeals to a broad range of people. Between Tucker-Grace and Fiona, there's a very broad range.

"I hoped he would select a woman," Fiona is telling her. "And was thrilled when he chose your mother. She's very accomplished to be so young."

Tucker-Grace rubs her palms on her dress and lifts her chin some. "She's driven, that's for sure."

Based on Tucker-Grace's tone, I'm not thinking she believes that's a good thing. At least not today.

"Where do you go to school? I haven't seen you at All Saints. Have I?" I ask, knowing that if she walked our halls, I would've spotted her. There's no way I could miss her.

"Oh, I don't live here."

Fiona and I exchange a glance. Her not living in DC could be a problem. It may hint at a fracture in their small family unit.

"Did you not get an information sheet about me?" Tucker-Grace pulls folded up pages from her purse. "I sure did about you."

"I'm not one for homework." I snatch the papers from Tucker-Grace's fingers, having never seen our bios for myself.

I flip through the pages, wanting to see what it says about me. The photo is a headshot taken during a photo shoot at the start of the campaign. "Jack is an excellent student who excels in debate and takes part in several extracurricular activities." I flip the page to Fiona's. "Who writes this crap? Check this out, Fie." I read the first line from her bio. "Fiona Wright the adopted daughter of-" I look up at her. "Ever think there will be a bio where the fact you're adopted isn't the first thing they mention?"

Fiona rolls her eyes and chuckles, showing no sign of offense. "As if it isn't obvious."

I've always found it offensive but have never asked her if she feels the same. They don't start all of my biographies with: The biological child of..., so to always start off with Fiona's relation to the family must be more of a political reason than a personal one.

Tucker-Grace shrugs. "I don't know. You two look a lot alike. Practically twins."

Fiona smiles at the teasing and then rests her chin on her arm. "You don't live here?" She's back on point and doesn't even give Tucker-Grace a chance to adjust.

"Nope."

"Do you live with your father?" Fiona presses.

Tucker-Grace runs her finger through her blonde hair, causing those bracelets to jingle again. She untucks her hair from behind her ear and lets it fall in her face, partially hiding her from us. "I don't even know who my father is." I'm not sure, but I think there is shame in her voice. I regret our inquisition.

Fiona and I exchange another quick glance, and I know that Fiona is wondering if they vetted that portion of Josie's past. An unknown birth-father will get people talking and make some nervous.

My mom, especially.

"I live with my two aunts."

"Ah." Fiona's eyes light up. "The Vice-Presidential candidate's daughter lives with her married aunts. That will play well. People love the modern family angle."

"They aren't lesbians," Tucker-Grace corrects Fiona's assumption. "They're sisters."

Fiona's momentary jubilation dissipates. Two sisters

aren't as discussion worthy, and I can't help but laugh at her assumption.

"No lesbians in the family I'm aware of," Tucker-Grace says. "But I have a transgender distant cousin if that helps."

She's witty. I like it.

"Anyway, I was twelve when my mom won her Senate seat. I think no one expected her to win it so we didn't plan to be apart, but it happened, and she didn't want me in the mess of DC, so I stayed with my grandparents and aunts." She's rambling so she must be nervous. "Then, two years ago my grandparents died in a car accident and my aunt Elliot was sort of left to run the house in my mother's absence."

"I'm sorry to hear that," I tell her, with what I believe is genuine compassion, but I can't be sure because it's a foreign emotion for me.

"Then you must not see your mother often," Fiona says, with slightly less compassion than even I managed.

"She flies home every Thursday and stays until early Monday morning."

"Wow. So, you'll stay in Texas if she wins?" I ask.

"Oh yeah. For sure. DC's not for me." She eyes her dress. "Which I'm sure you two figured out."

If she wouldn't fit in, it wouldn't be because of her clothes. It would be because she isn't a fan of the game, and I expect she'll refuse to play it.

"I don't know." I sit back so I can watch her without being obvious. "We've got people from all backgrounds at our school. I mean, sure, we've got cliques just like every-where else, but we're the United Nations in miniature."

"All faiths, all backgrounds, all skin tones and orienta-tions," Fiona adds.

"And all issues," I say. "Issues you didn't even know were issues. Trust me, people can make something out of nothing and let you know you're wrong about your stance regarding it."

The SUV pulls into a spot at the front of the restaurant, momentarily bringing our conversation to an end. I wish the drive was longer, and we could continue to talk in a bubble without fear of someone overhearing.

I reach for my phone. It's a habit and doing it reminds me I've informed people we're coming. I glance out the window and see a few paparazzi hiding behind trees and cars. I'm back to hating myself for leaking the details of this early dinner.

With a technique that Fiona wouldn't be caught dead doing, Tucker-Grace bounds over the middle seat and is about to jump out the vehicle. I grab her by the arm and try to slow her exit, so she won't get outside and be ambushed alone.

"Allow me." I exit the vehicle and adjust my belt, so I have a second to eye our surroundings. They aren't moving in yet. I have a few seconds to whisk her inside before anyone approaches.

As my parents raised me to do, I offer my hand to assist Tucker-Grace in exiting the vehicle.

She stares at my hand, and I can imagine she's at war with herself. Sure, she doesn't need my help, but some could construe it as rude to deny the gesture. They could also consider it rude for me to offer help.

I wait. My heart rate escalates. If she denies me, it'll be photographed for the world to see. It will also mean that the small connection we've made is a figment of my imagination.

Tucker-Grace looks up, making eye contact with me. Like President Kirkland did back at the house, I stand firm, hold her gaze, and wait, hoping she'll accept my hand.

With a smirk, Tucker-Grace finally slips her hand into

mine. "Thanks, Jack." She tightens her grip on my hand and then climbs out of the vehicle.

We stride towards the entrance. She pulls her hand away from mine. I must have weaved my fingers through hers in such a natural movement I didn't realize I'd done it until she slipped hers out from between mine.

"I'm sorry," I mutter, checking her eyes for a sign of offense. "The hand holding thing. It was an accident."

She smiles, and her eyes hint more at amusement than affront. "No problem. It's been a weird day."

I open the door, stand back and study my hand as Tucker-Grace enters the restaurant. The sensation in my fingers has left me shook. She's affected me, and if she's elicited this response from me in less than an hour, I'm genuinely curious what she'll bring out in the next six months.

11

FIONA

WITH JACK and Tucker-Grace out of the vehicle and the driver waiting outside as I requested, I'm in the vehicle by myself.

My stylist and hair and make-up team were with me when I was getting ready, so this is the first moment I've been alone today, and it's incredible.

I pull out my phone and see that I've missed calls from Austin but can't return them right now. I open the Instagram app, and search for Tucker-Grace. Before I even click on her profile, I see the blue check mark. They have verified her, which leaves me conflicted. I know it's necessary, but seeing the blue check gnaws at me. and I can't pinpoint why.

My jaw clinches tight as I scroll through Tucker-Graces photographs. In each, she's playful, always beautiful and relaxed.

It's infuriating and unfair, and I can now pinpoint my emotions about it. I'm envious.

Envious that her mother didn't drag her into her political life and push her front and center.

She's about to enter our world, but I wish it were the other way around.

I pull a compact from my purse and stare back at myself through the small mirror. I look old. Far too old and far too hard for only being sixteen. In a fight to keep my tears at bay, I take several deep breaths. I look at myself for several long seconds and try to will my skin to smooth and my eyes to soften. My efforts are in vain, however.

I startle at movement out of the corner of my eye.

Photographers surround the vehicle in the blink of an eye. They snap photos and yell my name.

Remember when we got to be free like that. I try to drown the paparazzi out.

I consider my question, but the answer comes quickly. *No. Me either.*

My soul is constricted by the weight of the world watching my every move. Although I'm growing to love it, this isn't the life I would have picked for myself, and I wonder if Tucker-Grace, now presented with a public life as an option, will choose it for herself.

I would advise her against it, but so far, she hasn't asked my opinion.

"One… two… three… four… five…" In therapy for the last few years, my counselor has me using different relaxation techniques and tools to improve my mental health.

I now allow myself ten seconds to feel. In this situation, ten seconds to grieve the loss of the life I never had. "… eight… nine… ten."

With a sharp inhale, I collect myself, straighten my blouse, and climb out of the vehicle. Always prepared, I put on a large smile and wave.

Back to business.

12

TUCKER-GRACE

THE RESTAURANT IS ULTRA-TRENDY. Thin strips of light meant to resemble bamboo line the walls and cast a light green sheen over the slick table surfaces. The green of the chopsticks, laid on white cloth napkins, matches the lighting. Instrumental music plays through the sound system.

Overhead, elegant tiny lights simulate stars. Outside, people shout our names through the glass doors. Someone must've alerted them we were coming, which is new to me, but I realize it won't be weird for long. It'll be the norm in a matter of days.

If I were visiting the restaurant under different conditions and without people watching or photographing every second, I think I'd actually like it.

Fiona and Jack stop at a large aquarium that separates the public and private eating areas.

After a minute of enjoying the salt-water fish in the tank, the waiter leads us to the back of the restaurant, and I'm relieved to see that we'll be able to eat in peace. Relieved, until I see the photographers pressed up against the windows outside. They're trying to shove each other out of the way so they can get a shot. The lenses of their cameras are hitting the glass. It sounds like when birds fly up to our windows back home and tap their beaks on the glass. It's unnerving, and I more resemble that goldfish back in my room than I ever thought I might.

"Please," the waiter encourages. "Have a seat."

I force my attention away from the chaos outside. I'm the only one still standing. Fiona and Jack are already seated and looking up at me like they're trying to figure out if I'm staying, or I'll make a run for it.

Honestly, I'd rather make a run for it, but escape isn't an option.

With my heart racing, I slip into the seat, pick up the cloth napkin, and place it on my lap before I look around.

The waiter places bowls of miso soup down in front of us. Not what I would've ordered, but I'm not up for eating, anyway. My stomach is in knots, and the thought of eating anything makes it tighten even more. My nerves are getting the best of me. Sitting next to two of the most spectacular individuals I've ever met — two people so perfectly put together and well-rehearsed — well, I'm petrified.

I search for a menu but don't spot one.

"May I get you something to drink?" The waiter asks, startling me of my bout of self-loathing.

"Iced tea," Fiona requests.

"Sparkling water for me," Jack says.

"Dr. Pepper," I order, out of habit.

"No, ma'am," the waiter says. "We don't carry Dr. Pepper."

"No, Dr. Pepper? Wow, okay. Sweet tea then, please."

He presses his lips together and sighs. "No. I can bring an iced tea and you may add as much sugar as you'd like." He doesn't even attempt to hide the fact he's talking down to me.

I'm now embarrassed and want the moment over so I go for the safest and easiest thing I can think of. "I'll take water."

"Sparkling or bottled?" Now he's playing games. Trying to make me feel smaller. Which is working. All eyes are on me. My chest tightens and aches, and my mouth goes dry.

I'm suddenly parched. "Plain water."

"With lemon?"

All I can manage is a shake of my head.

The waiter spins around and walks away. As he goes, Jack calls out, "Thanks for your hospitality there, man."

"Wait!" I wave for the waiter, but he's gone and I'm still sitting here without a menu.

"Jerk," Jack says under his breath, which I appreciate, but Fiona must not because she slaps his elbow.

I look around for the waiter so I can request a menu, but when I don't catch sight of him, I dive right into questioning the sibling. "Why is the President such an ass?"

Jack, who was just about to take a sip of soup, lowers his spoon back to the bowl and grins over at me. His blue eyes stand out against the blue of his shirt. "Great question."

Fiona rests the soup spoon on the bowl, clasps her hands and looks over at me. "President Kirkland has the highest favorability rating of any former sitting president."

"Because they haven't witnessed what I just did," I tell her.

Jack shoves his bowl out of the way and places his forearms on the table edge. "The highest favorability ratings in skewed polls."

Fiona lowers her brow and lightly sucks in her cheeks, revealing amazing bone structure. "People like him, Jack."

"People who like war-mongers and divisive leaders who

pit citizens against each other," he answers. His thinking is far more aligned with mine than his own sister's.

She scowls even more. "He's likable."

"Not from what I just watched."

"His policies are terrible," Jack continues. "Look at what he's done to the Democratic Party." He turns his attention to me again. "That man is so narcissistic he doesn't see his culpability in the failings of the party at all. He points the finger at everyone but himself."

"Jack, the economy is steady."

I can't fight the urge to offer her a different point of view, so I do. "Ask middle America if they would agree with that statement."

"Exactly," Jack tells his sister, before turning to me and pretending to whisper. "She's colorblind. Can't see red."

"Cut it out," Fiona warns playfully, over his assertion that she doesn't see the views of those living in predominately Republican states. Only I don't think he was teasing.

The waiter sets down the drinks. "They ordered your food prior to your arrival, and it will be here shortly."

My nagging curiosity why the waiter didn't give us menus when we sat down is now answered, and I'm left wondering what someone ordered for me to eat. This early dinner will be filled with surprise and mystery, and I despise both.

This campaign, should it happen, may see me losing some freedom and anonymity. Heck, I'm even losing my ability to choose my own meals, and nobody even asked me what I like. I doubt they care.

Unfazed, Jack squeezes his lemon wedge into his glass and takes a sip of water. "People believe the two-party system has failed them."

"It has failed them." I take a sip of what I'm guessing is

tap water. "Some would say it's time for a revolution."

"Our father would like to unify the country. Slice through the two-party narrative and go straight to the American people with a message of unity and strength."

It sounds like Fiona's spouting talking points, and she's really, really good at regurgitating them. Although it's impressive, it's not a skill I care to gain. What I'd like to know if she wants the same thing he does, but I don't think she'd tell me if she didn't.

"There isn't a sane person on the planet who thinks it'll work," Jack says.

"Dad believes it will work. He wouldn't run otherwise. He sees the Rust Belt, Florida and Nevada turning purple." The more she speaks, the more in command she seems. "Have you seen Dad's numbers? Pollsters say he'll jump at least ten points just off the news of adding Josephine to the ticket."

I rub my temples. A headache is coming on. Math and numbers have never been my thing. And nothing could be more boring than talking statistics.

"Ten points from what," Jack asks her. "He's at ten percent. That won't get him elected, and it won't get us to two-seventy."

Fiona shrugs as she eyes her phone. "True, the Electoral College will be more challenging."

"Correction winning the Electoral College is an impossibility." Jack sits back, takes another drink of water and sloshes it around in his mouth before swallowing. Almost like the topic of discussion left a bad taste in his mouth.

He looks to me again. The boy has amazing eye contact, and I wonder if it's something they've taught him. "Republicans are just as bad as the Democrats. There isn't a likable candidate in the race."

"Why would your dad run as an Indy? And why would President Kirkland support it? This whole thing doesn't make a lick of sense."

Again, Fiona leans forward and rests her forearms on the table. "President Kirkland wants to continue to be the face of the party. He can't do so if my father runs as a Democrat."

"So…" I'm putting all the pieces together, albeit slowly. There's so much going on behind the scenes that normal people like me never know about. It's a little awe-inducing when you get a peek behind the curtain. "The president is willing to —"

"He's not willing. This is his idea entirely," Jack says. "Allow the Democrats to fall on their face so he can rush back in and save the day. Or so he thinks. He knows that no matter who the Democratic candidate is, they won't win."

"Because the people are pissed." It's a total guess on my part.

Jack looks at me with a large grin and wide, excited eyes. "Exactly."

I'm shocked that I'm putting this together and getting it right. Maybe I'm better at this political stuff than I gave myself credit for.

Jack's intensity grows. "From what I've heard Dad and his team say, Kirkland thinks he'll allow the Republicans to have the presidency so they can take the country further into recession and leave us in a… he uses air quotes. "…quagmire in the middle east." He sits back, but quickly sits right back up, reengaged. "After the Republicans screw everything up, Kirkland can help rebuild the Democratic Party. The man literally thinks he controls not only a presidency and Congress, but the people too." Jack shakes his head in disgust. "It's sick. He's sick."

"Kirkland doesn't think my father will win the election,"

Fiona continues. "But neither will the Democratic candidate. It's not in the cards this time around, but he believes our father can come back in four years and explain to the people he ran as a third-party candidate because he heard their cries." She takes a sip of water and continues. "My father can convince the American people that he believes the Democratic Party is back on track and is again the true party of the people. When he comes back, he brings a brand-new and energized contingency with him. What Kirkland doesn't know is that my father believes the current version of both parties will soon be a thing of the past. They've lost touch with much of the country."

"And he'll lead the way into a changed political party system," I mutter, finally putting the pieces together in something that makes sense. Scary sense, but sense.

If this insanity works, my mother won't just be the first female vice president; she'll be one half of the first independent ticket ever elected.

"So, your dad and the President are using each other?"

"That's how the game is played," Fiona says with a shrug.

Jack stirs his ice water again, but this time with his straw, and looks over at me with a sly grin. "It's how the game is played."

It's crazy that they can look at this like it's a game. For me, it's not a game. It's my life, but at the moment, I'm nothing more than a token being moved around a game board.

A flash of a camera strobe. I nearly jump out of my skin. Jack reaches over and places his hand on my arm. "You okay?"

I nod. The cameras continue to flash. I'd somehow forgotten they were there.

The waiter places several sushi rolls onto the table.

As I reach for my glass of tepid water, I see my hands are

shaky. The manipulation of the system… and the people has me more freaked out than ever.

I glance at the photographers.

"Do you ever get used to all this attention?"

"Tucker-Grace," Jack says with some sympathy. "If we ever get used to it, that's when we'll have problems."

"But it gets a little easier to accept," Fiona adds as she picks up her chopsticks.

I start to grab a piece of sushi with my fingers but stop. Photographers are observing me from outside the window. Fiona and Jack use their chopsticks with no problem. I pick up a pair, perch them between my fingers and try to conform, but fail miserably and reach a further level of embarrassment. "I've never been good at these things," I mutter, covering my humiliation.

Fiona and Jack watch me struggle with the use of chopsticks. It's more difficult under the weight of their stares. With each failed attempt, my frustration intensifies, and the paparazzi take more photographs.

Jack throws down his chopsticks and picks up a piece of sushi with his fingers. We share a smile before he shoves the entire piece into his mouth. I appreciate that he's willing to sink to my level, so I'm not so alone.

I follow his lead and stuff a piece of sushi in my mouth, but not as neat.

Jack reaches over and wipes a piece of rice from my face as the cameras outside the windows flash. My face heats up, and I can't tell if it's from embarrassment or his touch.

Jack hands me a fork. "Know how to use one of these?"

I yank the fork from his fingers, amused by his playfulness. "I think I can manage."

Jack grins. "Me or the fork?"

I stab the sushi roll. "Both."

13

GRASSROOTS. FASHION

Hello, world!

Let's get straight to business and head over to the clothesline.

The Clothesline:

I just got word that someone spotted our lovely Fiona Wright at Sushiniko in downtown Arlington with both Jack and... are you ready for this? Tucker-Grace Bishop.

The "It Girl" of the day.

Since the unofficial announcement of her mother's

selection as Quaid Wright's running mate this morning, TG (as I'll call her, cause that girl's name is long!) has been trending number one on Twitter. Both her Twitter and Instagram feeds have grown to over a million. In less than a day!

The Closet:

I know that this blog is all things Fiona Wright, but I may just have to make an exception and include TG if she will be on the campaign trail.

Her style is so fresh and alive that I suddenly wish my entire wardrobe was boho chic.

I'd happily raid both of their wardrobes.

Today at dinner, Tucker-Grace wore a flowing floral above the knee dress with full-length arms that billowed at the wrist, and — get this — knee-high suede boots. Jaw droppingly amazing!

I'm in love.

Fiona was more classically dressed in a pair of tuxedo slacks and a polka-dot short-sleeved blouse.

You know how much I love Fiona, but she may just have to up her game if she will be standing next to Tucker-Grace all the time.

To see their fashion, head over to my post at: https://www.grassroots.fashion/post/a-meet-and-greet-for-the-ages.

The Swoon:

From the photos that I've seen, Jack is looking all kinds of smitten with the girl from Texas, and I'm thinking he's hoping TG will lasso his heart.

If so, do you think she can tame him? Do we want him tamed? Now THAT is the question of the day.

The Wrap:

I've never been a big fan of politics, but if these three will hit the campaign trail together, I may suddenly have to volunteer on the campaign.

Want to join me?

14

THE FOUR SEASONS is pretty amazing.

None of my bedrooms throughout my life could be more different from the one I'm sitting in right now. It's so much fancier than anything I've ever stepped foot in before. Unless you count the US Capitol Building the day, they swore Mom into the Senate.

The fabrics in the room are cream or a light green color. The brochure Helen gave me calls the colors vanilla and celadon. Very upscale sounding, but in terms of elegance, the fancier terms suit it better than my generic choices which would've been creamer and celery.

The worn-out Dallas Cowboys pajamas I brought to wear don't compliment the room and are out of place. Par for the course for the way the day has gone. I would look more appropriate in silk pajamas or a plush robe. But I wouldn't be myself.

Mom enters the room with curlers in her hair sweatpants and a button-up shirt that she can remove without messing up her hair once it's done.

She looks around and slinks over to me like she's about to share a big secret. "Isn't this fabulous?"

I run my hand over the plush 'vanilla' comforter and lean back into the cloud-like pillows. "Someone could convince me." I close my eyes and try to conceive of a life where these surroundings are the norm, rather than saved for a special occasion. "Putting us in a room called the East Wing Presidential Suit was a little on the nose."

"We may have to share a bed, but I thought it would bring good luck. The Wrights are getting ready in the West Wing Presidential Suit."

I laugh. "Of course, they are."

"Doesn't this take you back to the good old days?" We sprawl out on the king-sized bed that we're gonna share if we end up staying the night after the fundraiser and possible announcement.

Sharing a bed takes me back to the days when we lived alone in military housing. I always had my own room but being so far from home we preferred to stay close. Every night after dinner and my bath, we'd climb into bed and read books together. Just thinking about it comforts me some.

Mom always chose books that showcased girls being whatever they wanted or true stories about women who'd overcome the odds and accomplished something great.

I always believed Mom chose the books because the messages might inspire me to greatness. With my eyes now open to the world, I'm wondering if the books were more for Mom as a nightly impartation of strength and encouragement. It was Mom who had big dreams and wanted to accomplish something tremendous, and I'm just along for the ride.

"How was dinner?" Mom asks.

Bringing up the dinner causes the comfort from just a few

seconds ago to evaporate. "It was fine. I thought they'd be pretty uptight, but they weren't bad."

"Friendly?"

"Yeah."

"Encouraging?"

I don't have the heart to tell her that half the Wright duo thinks the Wright/Bishop journey towards the Presidency is ill-fated and will end in bitter disappointment.

"Absolutely." I despise lying to her, but if I were honest, she would blow off Jack's doubt, anyway. She's decided and telling her that there is doubt looming would only make me seem like a wet blanket trying to throw myself on her parade.

I roll onto my stomach and perch my chin on my hands. "It's weird though, ya know. There were so many cameras. We were just trying to have a meal, but I could hardly concentrate on getting to know Fiona and Jack better because out of the corner of my eye, all these people were snapping pictures. How do people live like this all the time? It didn't even feel safe."

"Funny you mention that." She sits on the corner of the bed and lays back so we're facing each other. "I'm sure you've noticed all the Secret Service agents around here."

"Who could miss them?" They look completely out of place. Even for DC.

"Some of them are here from Quaid's Advance Team. They're planning everything to the second but the others, well... they're here for us."

I flip around and sit back up, ready to hear more.

"Usually Vice-Presidential candidates aren't assigned a detail this early, but the Secretary of Homeland Security determined that you and I should receive Secret Service starting now."

The statement shoots a hole into my gut. "Is it really that dangerous?"

"Probably not, but it can't help to be cautious." Mom walks to the doorway. Her walk is different. As a soldier, she hoofed it everywhere in a modified march that pulled her shoulders forward like she was about to charge forward. Now, her shoulders are back, and her chin is slightly raised. Her posture is perfect, like Fiona and Jacks.

She's gone so much that I didn't notice the transformation before. DC has changed her more than I thought, and it makes my heart hurt.

She waves someone to her. "There's someone I need to introduce you to."

Another person. Wow. I've already met at least a dozen new people and will struggle to remember their names.

I scoot to the edge of the bed as a handsome man walks into the room. Grey streaks tinge his hair, and his dark eyes stand out against his clean-shaven, tanned face. He's wearing a black suit. Obvious Secret Service.

"This is Hyatt Westbrook. He's the Secret Service agent in charge of your security."

My security. Even with all the Secret Service around, I hadn't even imagined that one would be assigned to me.

"He'll be with me?"

Mom nods.

"All the time?" My stomach flips.

Her face scrunches a little. "He will."

I'm weirdly starting to panic. My freedom is slipping away from me. "But if you win, he won't live with me in Texas, right?"

"I'll leave you two to chat." She slinks a few steps away.

"Mom-" It's an attempt to avoid the topic. More bad news is circulating on the horizon. The changes just keep coming.

I'm sicker to my stomach. "If you win, I'll stay in Texas with Elliot and Sawyer. Right?"

Mom halts, returns and sits back down beside me. "You saw that huge house. You want me to live there all by my lonesome?"

My heart drops into my already hemorrhaging gut. My life is gonna change so much. She's already asking so much of me. "You're gonna ask me to move here?"

Her face practically melts, obviously hurt by my reaction. "Don't you want to be together?"

"I've wanted to be together for four years, but you became a US senator who lived half a country apart, so…" I allow the story to trail off. No sense in hashing up old wounds. Especially not in front of Hyatt.

"I'm doing what I believe is best for our family. All of our family."

I surrender a little. Mom carries the burden of helping to provide for her younger sisters and me and that's a lot. She doesn't need me piling on.

"Tuck, we'll discuss it if the time comes."

My anger returns and is already at a near boil. "No, Mom. This is the kinda thing you discuss before you get so far into it you can't go back."

Mom eyes the room and with a tilt of the head, beckons me to do the same. "Don't you think we're already to that point?"

She traipses into the living area like a child escaping their room on Christmas Eve so they can try to catch Santa Claus in the act but left their skeptical sibling behind to try to go back to sleep.

Did she not tell me about her nomination so that by the time I found out we'd be so far down the road I would be forced to go along with it?

It's starting to feel like that was the plan.

I'm reeling but try to contrive a smile. I look up at my new prison guard. "Nice to meet you, Hyatt."

"You too, Tucker-Grace." In comparison, his smile appears genuine. Fatherly, even, which is a foreign concept to me.

"Sorry, you're getting stuck with me. I'm sure I'll be the least interesting of the bunch."

"Maybe so." He leans against the door jam. He's far less formal than when you see them on television, all stiff and focused. "I'm hopeful though."

"Oh yeah? Why's that?"

"You're a Cowboys fan."

I perk up. The seizing in my gut lessens. "You too?"

"Of course not. Redskins all the way. At least we have something to talk about. Football is a universal language."

Now with a boost to my spirits, I smile again. This time, I didn't have to coax it into existence. "I love to talk about football."

"Texas girls usually do. Your mother raised you right." He stands to his feet and walks towards the door. "I'll let you get ready for the reception."

"Thanks." I look out the window at the view of the quaint and inspiring town of Georgetown.

"By the way, something to ponder. I need you to choose a codename starting with a B."

"Oh, yeah?" I look back at him with some curiosity. "Did my mom pick hers yet? If not, I have a suggestion."

He chuckles and raises an eyebrow. "They have to be longer than five letters and be at least two distinct syllables."

I appreciate that he already gets my sense of humor and bend toward a potty mouth when I feel so inclined. And I'm inclined. "I'm from the South. I can make any word have two distinct syllables."

"I'm sure you can."

"What did she choose?"

"Bluebonnet."

"Our state flower? Really?" So predictable. I sigh. "I'll think about it. When do you need an answer?"

"Before we head downstairs." He pushes off the door, about to leave the room. "Great to meet you, Tucker-Grace. It'll be an honor to work with you." I'm no expert, but based on his accent, I'm guessing he's from North Dakota or somewhere nearby.

"You too." He's around the corner when I call out to him. "Hey, Hyatt."

His head appears around the doorway. "Yes?"

"Would you take a bullet for me?"

"Let's hope we never find out." With a wink, Hyatt disappears into the crowd in the living room, and I already have a sense that he would take a bullet for me —and without hesitation.

Liz walks in carrying a hanging clothes bag. "Not that I don't adore what you brought with you, but…"

My shoulders slump again and the weight of the looming event returns. "Honestly, I can dress myself."

"I know you can, but you might want to at least consider this option."

Swooning, she hangs the outfit on a hook on the back of the door and clasps her hands over her heart. "It's Diane von Fürstenberg."

I don't know who that person is, but just the name has my curiosity peaked. I slide off the bed and walk towards the mysterious bag.

"I feel like it suits you perfectly. Not a suit, not a dress, but…" she unzips the bag.

I suck in a breath at the sight of the jumpsuit. "You're. Freaking. Kidding."

Liz slips her hand inside and pulls luxurious fabric outside the bag. "Metallic velvet."

I cover my mouth with my hands and bounce up and down. She has better taste than I gave her credit for, and I can't even imagine wearing something so amazing. I'm staring at an outfit that in my real life, I would never have the opportunity to wear, and it's the first thing about this trip that leaves me thrilled.

"It's way too low cut for an event like tonight's but if you put it with this black silk camisole and cover up the girls, it will still look stunning."

In shock and adoration, I step toward the jumpsuit and run my hand along the striped, wide pant leg. "Liz, it's stunning."

"See, I'm not a total Debbie Downer."

I hop over and hug her. "Thank you!"

"You need to feel confident out there on that stage. And this… wow, this will make you confident."

I ogle over the golden-colored fabric, then suddenly sober up. "Wait? On stage?"

15

"MOTHER, PLEASE. OPEN THE DOOR."

My father and Jack pace the room as I knock on the door for the tenth time, possibly more.

After twenty years of marriage, he has lost his patience for her bouts of crippling anxiety. I used to think his lack of compassion was cruel, but now understand that he hasn't lost compassion at all, he just doesn't feel any in return. And the constant need for attention becomes overwhelming.

I want to leave her in there. I'm exhausted from her demands and her brokenness is selfish. The timing of her episodes is suspect. It's not the fundraising or public events that cause her anxiety. She's accustomed to them and thrives on the attention.

These outbursts happen when my father is suddenly swimming in attention or positive press, and I believe they are a childish ploy to gain some attention from her high school sweetheart.

But he isn't the one who gives her attention. I'm left with the duty because I'm the only one who still has the fortitude to jump into the madness.

I stare at the doorknob as if I can somehow will it to unlock and open on its own, but my attempt at telekinesis is failing and we're running out of time. The event has already begun downstairs.

My phone vibrates. I check the screen and see that it's Austin. Unable to answer, I lower the phone back and lean against the door.

"Let me help you," I urge. I divert my eyes to my brother.

"Want me to try?" he asks. I appreciate his offer, but he's too soft with her and her episodes last longer. I've found the ability to pull her out more quickly and tonight, time is of the essence.

I shake my head and look back at the knob. "Open the door." I'm now making a command. My patience is running out.

The door unlocks and slowly swings open. I slip inside the bathroom and shut the door behind.

Inside the marble bathroom, my mother sits in a ball on the floor. She's clutching her hands to her chest and is breathing rapidly. The designer-suit her stylist selected is in a clump in the corner.

At another time, I would try to soothe her. Tonight, she's got to snap out of the fog, and she needs to do it quickly.

I pick up the dress, drape it on the hanger on the back of the door and turn on the shower hot water hoping the steam might release the new wrinkles.

"It's okay." I kneel beside her. "I'm here. Look at me." I wait for her to make eye contact.

Her grayish blue eyes eventually meet mine.

"Good, just take a deep breath. Breathe with me." Now overseeing the rebuilding of my mother's grit, I slowly inhale and watch her follow my lead. When my lungs are full, I slowly exhale. My mother mimics me. I cringe. There is alcohol on her breath.

I almost vomit.

"You're drunk?" She must've snuck the drink into her room when her team was prepping her for the night.

My mother wipes her face with the back of her hand. More child-like than political prodigy. "I- I need my medication."

"Mother, you've been drinking. That's not-"

She closes her hand into a fist and thrusts her neck forward, almost ramming her head against my shoulder. "I need my medication."

Mixing medication and alcohol is dangerous, and I'm worried it'll only cause more problems later. But I further understand that to put up a fight would be a useless endeavor.

I stand, place my phone on the counter, snatch a crystal glass off the counter, fill it with water and present it to her.

My mother reaches out with a trembling hand and retrieves it as I shake a pill out of the bottle and onto the counter and break it in half. "Just half of one."

Without looking at my mother, I pick up the pill half, hold out my hand, and ashamed to be further enabling her behavior, wait to feel her take it from my fingers.

She swallows down the medication, turns a half-circle and sits back against the wall as I pour a cap full of mouthwash and hand it to her.

Mother pours the green liquid into her mouth, swishes it around and then spits it back into the lid. I pour it down the drain, rinse the lid out and leave it on the counter to air-dry.

I used to resent this duty, but I've now accepted the role. Instead of ignoring her, like my father often does, I think back to a day when I was struggling with the pain of being abandoned by my birth-mother. It was my sixth birthday and as every birthday seems to do; it had me thinking more about my birth mother than my family. I wanted her to come and get me, or I wanted to believe that she at least wanted to.

I'd created a full story in my head. She wanted to have me back, but my parents wouldn't let her. It was easier to make them the bad guys. It somehow hurt less.

Frustrated and fed up, I announced that I was running away to find her. I packed my American Girl doll suitcase and went to sit on the curb outside in hopes of someone picking me up and taking me to a woman who had never held me in her arms.

I'd only been outside for a few minutes before I heard a strange noise behind me. The sound scared me at first. I thought someone bad was coming to get me, but when I turned to investigate, I found my mother walking towards me and dragging a full set of luggage with her.

"What's that?" I asked her.

My mother pulled up beside me and steadied her bags. "My luggage. I love you and if you're running away, I'm going with you." She sat down on the curb next to me and looked up and down the street as if she was expecting a car to pull up any second.

I stared at her for a long while trying to figure it out. How could she love me so much? I wasn't hers. I didn't look like anyone in my family. I often threw tantrums and refused her affection. How could she possibly want to run away with me, and why wouldn't she simply let me go? If she would, her life could be so much easier.

Another sound pulled my attention to the driveway where my father and Jack pulled suitcases of their own. I was more surprised than ever, and I couldn't understand why they would want to come with me.

"Why are you all coming?"

My mother gazed down at me with more love than I've ever witnessed. "Because we're a family and that will never change. So, if you're going somewhere, we're all going with you."

The four of us sat on the curb surrounded by our luggage for several minutes, and when a car never stopped to pick us up, I made the decision that maybe I wouldn't run away.

I believe that I fully bought in to our family that day, and I stopped putting up a fight. The tantrums stopped, and I fell in line. Still to this day, when things go haywire and life is unfair, I have to make the same commitment. I won't run away. Physically or emotionally.

Not like she so often does.

My phone vibrates on the sink. I don't have to look to know it's Austin. As much as I'd love to hear his voice, I need to wait for my mother's anxiety to lessen and the steam to fill the room. Like that day out on the curb, she's loaded down with baggage, and even though I'm left with another heart-crushing duty, I'm not about to let my mother face the world alone.

16

"… We have a reception on the George Washington Terrace, followed by the formal announcement in the Grand Corcoran ballroom."

The room is full of people. I've tried to remove myself from the drama and against everyone's advice, I'm scrolling through the Twitter feed. Photos of Jack and me at dinner are flooding the stream in a wave of drama that makes me sick to my stomach.

"Are you ready for all of this?" Mom asks me over her shoulder. "It's a big night."

My cell phone vibrates, preventing me from having to lie and say I can't wait to get downstairs. I check the screen and see it's Cody. I want to be excited to answer and have someone to talk to so I'm not so alone, but my fear is that he's seen the photos as well, and he's bought into the narrative that Jack and I are into each other.

"It's time," Stella announces.

Unfortunately, Cody's call will have to wait.

I swallow down the bile rising in my throat. Between the photos, Cody, and the hundreds of influential people from the list I studied earlier, the night is full of uncertainty and intense amounts of pressure.

Mom walks to me and briefly squeezes my hand. "Here we go." She squeals a little like a bride on her wedding day. "I can't believe this is happening."

I coerce a smile. From the moment earlier in the day that I realized Mom was hoping to be the Vice President, to now — staring out the window and looking out across Washington DC, I know there's nothing my mother has ever wanted more.

I thought it was nothing more than a passing pipe dream or a whim to Mom, but it's obviously so much more. I'm nauseous.

I look over my shoulder and watch everyone exit the room. Hyatt stands at the door, waiting for me to follow. He's now serious and on task.

I emotionally ready myself and then walk across the room and into the hallway.

As I exit, Hyatt says: "Bohemian is on the move."

The two-sided tape holding my top in place, so I won't reveal too much is a little itchy, but I try to ignore it as we walk down the hallway and stand outside the elevator.

I look over at my mom. I want to grip her by the arm and tug her down the hall towards the emergency stairwell. This is it. Our chance to escape before it's too late. We can run off right now, and the Vice-President could just tell everyone that the leak was wrong. She was never his choice.

But she's bought into it, and there's no escaping. When the elevator opens, and we step inside, we're committed to entering a new world.

The doors open.

My heart drops.

The Wrights are all standing inside. Smiles on their faces and looking down-right jaw-dropping.

They're really fantastic at this.

Jack's wearing a slim fit black suit with a thin tie and looking at the floor numbers above.

Fiona gasps at the sight of me. "Oh, my word, that is spectacular."

"Thank you, Fiona." It's nice to have her approval.

Mom steps into the elevator. As I follow, Jack lowers his gaze and locks his eyes on mine. When he looks at me, he almost looks like he's staring directly into the sun. His eyes tighten at the corners with a stern glare. I quickly lower my gaze, step into the elevator, and move to the back.

Out of the corner of my eye, I watch Jack look back up at the numbers, curious why making eye contact with him makes me so uneasy. Maybe because I couldn't tell by his expression if he approved of the outfit or not. Not that it matters. Maybe I sensed anger or resentment in the tight corners of his eyes.

He seems to change between highly engaged and aloof.

Jack Wright. He's a mystery.

I look back to Fiona, who is exactly what I would expect. Perfectly put together and polite. Whether her friendliness is earnest, I have no way of knowing. At least not yet.

"I love your dress," I tell her. "Everything you do seems so effortless." She's in a form fitting navy blue dress that looks flawless on her, but on me, every flaw would glare like a spotlight was shining directly on them.

"You got it right when you said 'seems'," Jack says, with a brief look at me over his shoulder.

As we wait for our ride to end, I glimpse the Wrights and then Mom. She seems to fit better with them. My heart pings with a bit of an ache. I'm losing her.

The elevator chimes. Everyone smiles. I do the same but am not sure it translates as well for me as it does them.

The doors open and the show is on.

Staffers usher us down the hall to the event I read about on our schedule, on the George Washington Terrace. It's a night of schmoozing and fundraising. The schedule didn't include that description, but I know enough to know that's what I should expect. Unfortunately for my mom, I'm not good at schmoozing or fundraising. I wasn't old enough to take part when she ran for Senate, so this is all new to me.

Members of the Washington upper-class and their teen offspring, dressed in fashions that most of their constituents could never afford, snack on locally sourced hors d'oeuvres. Or at least that's what the sign at the entrance told me. And they're drinking wine by the barrel. In no time at all, these people are gonna be three sheets to the wind.

Secret Service agents flank the room and hover nearby as the Vice President, Mrs. Wright, Mom, and Fiona enter the patio and start to work their magic. I'm stuck at the door, unable to make myself walk inside.

The whole scene is too intimidating. I don't belong here.

I jump at the touch of something on the small of my back. I look over my shoulder. It's Jack. He puts his mouth to my ear. "The secret is to find somewhere you can observe the madness without wading into it."

He's a good four inches taller than I am, even when I'm in heels. Of course, his blue eyes fix on mine as soon as I lift my head to make eye contact. This is something I'll have to grow accustomed to, because as of right now, that kind of eye contact makes my chest flutter.

"You don't work a room?" It's the only question I could come up with, given the odd sensations racing through my body.

He smirks and his eyes soften as he removes his hand from my back. "Usually the room works me." He walks away and straight to a corner where he leans against a wooden post.

Girls instantly surround him. He's like royalty being entertained by his court and watching him smothered in so much attention, it's the first time I get any hint he isn't actually in his element. His chin is lowered, and he only looks up every once in a while.

He's playing with something in his hands. It's a nervous fidget. A tell.

Maybe I'm better at this than I thought.

His eyes flicker to mine.

I startle, and quickly avert my attention, caught. My face warms.

Embarrassed, panicked and alone, I search for my mom.

The pressure is immense, and the grand terrace is difficult to navigate. With every step, I bump elbows with someone or have to dodge another.

I spot her a few feet away, make my way over and grasp her elbow.

She turns and kisses me on the cheek. "There you are. I lost you." She grips my hand. "Actually, I was afraid you deserted me already."

"Don't think I didn't consider it."

She turns, and I follow her into the wave of questions and examination.

A man whose nose is red and his eyes blood-shot approaches and invades my personal space with a step too close. Uncomfortable, I step back and eye the room, looking for a way to escape. Instead, I see Hyatt just a few steps away, and his eyes wholly on me and the man.

Hyatt nods. I take it as a promise he'll descend upon the man in the blink of an eye if it becomes necessary. I'm safer than ever.

"Tucker-Grace, now that your mother is about to be the Vice President, what legislation would you like to see passed?"

Unable to tell if the man's question is a genuine interest or an attempt to stump me, I consider his inquiry. I could dive into a discussion about better treatment of our veterans, immigration, or the importance of environmental safety precautions for oil rigs in the Gulf of Mexico, but I don't trust that he might use anything I say against my mother, so instead, I take a different approach. "I'd like to see the NCAA football playoffs expand to eight teams instead of four."

The man chuckles, which only eggs me on.

"Keep the major bowl games, the Rose, Orange, Sugar, and Cotton, but turn them into playoff games so you don't lose those important financial corporate sponsorships or the added revenue that's brought to each city." As his eyes show more amusement, I pick up the pace. I'm on a roll and if he came for ammunition, he's not gonna get it. Unless he has something against football. But to some, that would be un-American. "The greater Los Angeles area, Miami, New Orleans, and Dallas see a huge increase in revenue for the week of the games. And mostly, fans would stay much more engaged for the entire season."

I try to maintain eye contact but just a few feet away the Vice President, in the middle of a conversation, eyes a brunette up and down as she passes. The sight guts me.

"Then…" The Vice President's behavior scrambles my thoughts, and I struggle to corral them back. "Then… um… send the winners of the four major conferences and take an additional 14 at large based on the Coaches and AP poll rankings. Seems to make more sense, and there would be less fighting every year about who truly deserves the championship."

"I don't think college football falls under our jurisdiction," the man tells me, with levity in his voice.

"I know," I say with a shrug, like I couldn't have come up with anything better. "But you asked."

"You just exhibited unusual political savvy, unknowingly camouflaged in football knowledge," he says before another chuckle.

"Really?" I'm shocked that my pile of dung impressed him. To thwart additional questions, I add a little extra. "Well, politics aren't really my thing, but Mom and I are a team. We include each other in everything we do and every decision we make."

Mom smiles over at me, fully knowing that the statement was a private dig. She laughs and looks back at the man. "So sweet, isn't she, Senator Cochran?"

Crap. He's a Senator. And I just talked about college football like some sorority girl at a frat party six drinks into trash can punch.

I want to slink away and must've pivoted to go without realizing it, because Mom gripped me by the arm and has tugged me back to her.

As she talks to another group of people, I take in the room. Naturally, I find Fiona and watch her at work just a few feet away. She's standing with her parents and nods her head, says a "wow" or "that's so interesting" or, "I believe we will do better in the future".

"Without the support of leadership, I don't know if I can donate," the woman is telling Vice President Wright.

Fiona slowly reaches us and scratches behind her ear and barely rubs her neck. Maybe she's not as comfortable at all of this as I initially thought.

"Hear me out, Rayna," he responds. "While it's true that

the leadership won't back me, the rest of the story is that the people no longer back them."

He's not holding back. I like it.

The woman's eyes widen, and she nods reluctantly, so he dives right back in. "It's difficult to hear, but it is the truth. We're looking at much of the country that those of us on the coasts have either ignored or insulted for far too long. They're willing to throw support behind anyone who will hear them out and look out for their best interests for a change."

"But someone has to lead the party," the woman argues.

The Vice President leans towards her, his eyes wide and alive. "I don't want to lead a party. I want to lead the people."

Impressive.

The guy is so good that I almost buy the crap he's shoveling. The man is gifted, and nobody can deny it.

He could actually win this thing. How terrifying.

"Fiona!" The high-pitched squeal of her name breaks through the crowd noise.

I scan the room to find two girls on their tiptoes and waving her over. They look to be our age. Actually, no. None of them look to be my age. They may be my age, but they surely don't look it. In the clothes, makeup and in these surroundings, they look more like twenty-four, and I'm more like a pre-pubescent wanna-be who doesn't really wanna be but thinks she should.

Fiona excuses herself with a polite nod and strolls away, taking her time and stopping to greet several possible donors on her way.

My FaceTime rings. It's probably Cody. He's usually practicing at the arena at about this time and if I'm not there in person, he likes to have me watch on FaceTime.

"Hey, you. Gimme a sec." I turn to Mom. "It's Cody. I need to take this. I'll be right back."

Fully in her element, she nods and goes right back to talking with another possible donor.

As I make my way out of the crowd, I hold my phone up and give Cody a good look at what he's missing. "This is pure craziness. I mean, have you ever seen anything so fancy?"

"Can't talk long. It's my turn up."

"I'm hurrying." I practically shove my way through the people and into the hall. "Sorry I haven't been able to pick up."

He removes his hat and wipes his brow. "Yeah. You look busy." His voice is a little biting and his jaw is tight, but he focuses on putting on his protective helmet.

"Yeah, Tuck." Rusty, a rodeo clown in the making, appears over his shoulder "Looks like your havin' some fun out there. We were looking at the pics on Twitter." Rusty spits his smokeless tobacco onto the dirt below. "TuckJack. What's that about?"

"It's a stupid hashtag."

Behind him, handlers shove a bull into the chute below.

"Here I go," Cody says.

"Cowboy up," I tell him.

He hands the phone over to whom, I don't know, and Cody follows the same routine he does every single time he rides.

He slips onto the bull, adjusts the grip, and continues through the steps. Each one feeds the energy and hostility between the bull and the rider.

After another adjustment of his legs around the bull's girth, Cody nods. My heart stalls. It always does just before he breaks out of the chute.

The gate flies open. The bull, whose rage matches Cody's, bucks its way out.

One.

The bull drops his right shoulder, throwing his wide body off center.

Two.

The bull spins back to his left. Kicks his hind legs into the air with a snap of his back.

Three.

He cranks his neck right. Cody flies into the air and falls to earth with a violent thud. My heart beats to life, but I'm crushed for him. He hates it when the bull wins.

Incensed, he rips the gloves off his hands and throws them on the ground, then jumps to his feet and retrieves the phone.

"Okay. About the pictures." When he doesn't respond, I continue with an explanation that isn't even necessary. "We were having dinner. We-"

"A very friendly dinner," he accuses.

He's whipping himself into a fit over nothing, but this is what we do. I'm used to it. "I wouldn't call it that. It was awkward, really. There-"

"Didn't look awkward to me."

"Cody, I was at a dinner with two people I know nothing about, and I was only there because I had to be."

He removes his helmet, wipes his brow, and shoves his cowboy hat back on. "How much more of this campaign stuff are you gonna do?"

"I don't know. This is all new to me too."

"You're the one that left me here wondering what's goin' on and with everyone asking me how I enjoy seeing you hanging all over another guy."

"Hanging all over?" I try to contain a laugh. His accusations are ridiculous.

"How am I supposed to answer them? It's embarrassing."

His selfishness is infuriating. "We aren't even officially together anymore. You owe no one an explanation about anything. Especially one about something as stupid as dinner with a guy and his sister."

His eyes bulge and looks around angry as he storms through the arena. "So that's how you're gonna play this? That we aren't officially together?"

"We aren't! You're the one that made that clear last week when-"

"We'll talk later."

The line goes dead, and I'm left staring at the phone in my hand in disbelief. "He hung up on me."

I spin around and make sure there are no witnesses before exploding into a profanity-laced tirade muttered hardly above hearing level and then walk away from the madness just a few feet away.

I don't have it in me to return and put on a show.

Neither love, politics, nor bull-riding is for the faint of heart.

17

FIONA

BRITTANY HODGES and Pia Anand save me from having to listen to my parents attempt to convert liberals and conservatives to a more middle of the road stance on just about everything. Or at least support his riding of the center line.

Brittany and Pia would call themselves my friends, but they're friends who are opportunists in disguise. With their parents in politics, 'ladies-in-waiting' would more aptly describe them than the term 'friends'.

In monarchies, ladies-in-waiting care for princesses and queens. In DC, a lady-in-waiting is someone literally waiting to take their turn at the top, and they'll do it forcibly if necessary.

"Look at you." I hug Brittany quickly. "So tan. How were the Turks?"

"Unbelievable. I wish you could have gone with us. The yacht was spectacular."

I release her and move to Pia, who is on her phone, but looks up in time to see me ready for a friendly embrace. "Did you see our pics?" she asks. "The water was so clear."

I pull away and look them over. Brittany's wearing a

Lilly Pulitzer shift dress. It's too casual for an event of this magnitude, but she's playing up the fact that she just returned from a trip to one of the most beautiful places on the planet. I can't blame her for wanting to prolong the feeling.

Pia is in Stella McCartney. Still very resort-wear looking, but formal enough for the night. The mint green color compliments her skin and doesn't look too different from the saris she often wears to the dinners her parents host.

The girls look happy and relaxed, and I'm envious that I wasn't able to go with them on their trip. I regret choosing to work on the campaign, but the optics of a presidential candidate's daughter frolicking on a private yacht would've been campaign ending.

"What did we miss?" Brittany asks.

"Nothing. Everyone's been gone on vacation for the most part."

"What about the Josephine Bishop news? That's huge."

I wondered how long it would take for them to question me about the surprise announcement. It didn't take long. "There is that."

"Why did you announce so soon?" Pia asks.

"We didn't it got leaked, but we'll make the most of it."

Pia steps closer. She's ready to get right to business. The business of gossip. "So? What's Tucker like?"

"During dinner, I asked if she was doing all right and all she said was 'yeah' and uh. The girl said six words and 'yeah' and 'uh' were two of them."

I bite my bottom lip, immediately regretting being so catty. When I'm around the other girls, I easily slip into pettiness like it's a pair of Jimmy Choo's.

It's also the price of admission to the group.

"Her posture is horrible, and she needs a better bra or a

boob job," Pia says, looking at her phone. "I mean, did you see her in that bikini?"

"You should introduce us so I can judge her for myself." Brittany tucks a strand of her faded pink hair behind her ear. "From what I've seen from reading her Instagram posts, she's practically illiterate. She literally uses the term *gonna*. That's not even a word."

Brittany has finally dropped the vocal fry, which used to tinge the end of her sentences. After one conversation with her, I'd want to wash out my ears and purge my mind of the sound.

"How are your appointments with your speech coach coming along, Brittany?" I ask. Her congressman father is running for a senate seat and she, too, is in campaign mode.

She rolls her eyes. "She's annoying. I have to repeat the same sentences repeatedly. So boring. Anyway, you have to introduce us to Tucker."

The fry returns, so I turn my attention away from her and search for Tucker-Grace. "Tucker-Grace must have escaped. You'll have to meet her later."

"Based on the pictures of dinner, Jack is smitten," Brittany says.

Brittany confirms my assumption that the blogs would edit the photos in a way that made them appear interested in one another. She peaked Jack's curiosity, but I'd never go so far as to call him smitten. "Jack's never smitten. Horny maybe, but never smitten." I glance around the room to ensure she or her mother won't hear. "He says he finds her interesting. Can you even fathom?" I roll my eyes for added effect. I mean the eye roll to convey that I don't take the opinions of bloggers or trolls seriously, but they're the pulse of the people. They're usually very in tune with the general thoughts of their audience, if not feeding their opinions to them to adopt as their own.

"Speaking of interesting, have you read the latest gossip about Austin Lee?" Pia asks.

"Austin?" Hearing his name causes my heartbeat to stall. "I saw nothing on Grassroots Fashion. What have you heard?"

Pia purses her lips and places her hands on her hips. "Tragic. You seriously haven't heard?"

I notice I'm fidgeting and attempt to control my panic. He'd called several times, but I didn't have the time alone to respond. "No, what?"

"He won't be back at All Saints next semester."

"Oh? Why?" Trying to calm myself, I stroke the side of my neck, but my stomach continues to churn and my chest aches.

"Police found his father passed out over on the Potomac Bridge this morning. Heroin overdose," Pia whispers. "It took two doses of Narcan to bring him to. Three doses to wake up the…" she glances around the room. "… hooker next to him."

My chest tightens further. Brittany dramatically gasps like it's the first time she's heard anything so horrid.

"That's nothing new," I say, attempting to lessen the melodrama. "Half the men in DC have done the same. It's just that nobody has caught them yet."

"True," Pia says. "But how many of those men were discovered while their wife was receiving chemotherapy treatment?"

Feeling smothered, I focus on my breathing and don't respond.

"And the rumor is that Senator Lee will take the family back to Charleston to give them." Pia uses air quotes, "Time to heal." With a roll of the eyes, she presses further. "Another juicy scoop: he already has a mistress put up in a condo back home."

"Have you ever considered that much of the gossip you hear isn't true?" The girls gasp at the gall of my statement. "How often are the rumors passed around about you true? And how often are they lies?"

Neither girl can answer without proving my point, so they remain silent. I'm never the one to speak out, and they're just as shocked by my defense as I am.

"Pardon me." I duck away and rush out of the room. Once around the corner, I pull my phone out of my clutch, dial, and allow it to ring several times before voice mail picks up.

"This is Austin. You know what to do." Hearing his voice causes my heart to ache. If the rumors are true, he's been left to deal with the weight of his father's actions all on his own.

"Austin, it's Fiona. I'm sorry I missed your calls. I just heard the news. I don't even know what to say. I-"

"Fiona."

A slight shiver runs down my spine, and my jaw tenses. I lower my phone, hide the screen against my stomach and look over my shoulder at my mother.

She has stuck her head around the corner. "People are wondering where you are."

"I stepped away for less than a minute. There's something I need to deal with."

"Please, we need you back." She snaps her fingers twice. The sound is like a severe sunburn to my soul.

Surrendering, I hang up the phone and follow my mother back into the storm.

18

JACK

"WHEN ARE we going to go out?" Sloan Hubbard rubs on my arm and spins her foot around on the tip of her toe. Every time she turns her leg to the left, it rubs against mine, which is the point. If arousal is her goal, she's failing. The sequins on her dress are tugging on my pants and grating my nerves.

My friends from school are standing to my left, talking political maneuvers like they think it'll get the attention of the girls. It won't. Unfortunately for them, their fathers aren't high enough on the totem pole to earn their attention, so their attempts to woo the ladies are in vain.

Out of the corner of my eye, I see Ava approaching. Sloan must have seen her too, and like a scared cat who believes they'll lose the war over territory, she and her friends slink away. The guys follow.

"Hey, Jack," Ava purrs.

I can't even make myself look at her and nothing about her assertiveness is helping. I still don't remember her from the night before and if she hadn't woken up in my bed this morning, I wouldn't recognize who she is now. By bringing her to the house, I mischaracterized my intentions, although I don't recall having any.

"Hey, Ava. Good to see you." It's a lie, but it's the polite thing to say.

"You too." She moves closer and slips her hands around my neck. My body tenses.

If roles were reversed, and I walked up to a girl and acted how Ava or Sloan have with me, I'd be labeled a predator.

I pry her hands away and check the room to make sure nobody is watching. Especially not Tucker-Grace. "Not the time or place. Tonight, it's about my father."

"Every night is about your father. Except maybe last night," she whispers in my ear, causing it to itch.

"Nope." I scratch my ear. "That was probably about my father, too."

"I thought maybe we could-"

She's expecting more, and I've got to cut it off before I cause her additional embarrassment when I refuse. "I don't think so, Ava. Things are crazy right now what with the campaign and all that goes with it." I push off the wall and walk away, heading straight for my Secret Service agent, Vinny. "Where's Tucker-Grace?"

Vinny speaks into his communication device. "Eyes on Bohemian?" He listens to the answer through his earpiece and looks back to me. "Douglass patio. Alone."

I exit the room and leave Ava in my wake.

When I step onto the Douglass patio, Tucker-Grace is sitting near the fire pit staring at the flames and deep in thought. Like she's wishing it would open a portal and take her away from the madness.

The people I just left inside thrive off public attention and crowds. For Tucker-Grace, it appears it's the opposite. They drain her of energy.

Hyatt walks up behind her and offers a bottle of water.

"Got anything stronger?" she asks, obviously in a sour mood.

Hyatt offers a cupcake instead.

"Perfect, thanks." She takes the pastry from his hand and gives it a full inspection.

I should probably leave her here alone to eat her cupcake and process whatever's running through her mind and has her so bothered.

But I can't.

I'm pulled to her. I caused this mess for her and if I can figure out a way, I need to help her through the minefield Fiona and I have already waded through.

Tucker-Grace peels the paper away from the cupcake as I walk up.

"Doesn't get much stronger than him," Hyatt says, loud enough for me to hear, before he backs away and joins Vinny several feet away.

"It seems my reputation precedes me." I wish it didn't, and I could somehow start our friendship with a clean slate.

"Yeah, pretty much everyone has warned me to stay away from you."

Disappointed in her response, I halt my approach. "Want me to leave?"

Tucker-Grace looks up at me with her large, doe-like green eyes and smirks. "Naw, I'm sure I can handle you."

With my heart racing, I walk around the fire pit and stand a few feet away as she pinches small pieces off the cupcake and tosses them into her mouth. Something tells me that if I weren't there, she would have shoved the entire thing into her mouth at one time, and I wish my presence wouldn't cause her to change that.

With so little control of her life, the girl should at least feel free enough to shove a full cupcake in her mouth if she so chooses.

"Let me guess, not a fan of crowds?"

She shrugs and looks over her shoulder in the terrace's direction. "I don't mind crowds, but I have an aversion to lying sacks of…" Almost like she's disgusted with herself, she winces and looks back at the fire. "Well, you get the point."

I study her for several seconds. The spirit I saw in her during the day has gone, and she's distant. My guilt for throwing her into the lion's den intensifies. "You're upset. Is it the announcement, the surprise, the people in there, or…"

She sighs. "I just got into a fight with my ex-boyfriend. I guess you and I made a splash on social media. He's beyond peeved."

I'm surprised by the answer. So many choices, and that's one I hadn't considered. "Do you mean because of all the pictures that are out there?"

She nods.

I look around, making sure nobody is watching through windows. "Why are you worried that he's upset if he's your ex?"

She holds up her cupcake like she's offering a toast at an elaborate dinner party. "And that, Jack Wright, is the question of the evening. Even better than someone asking me what legislation I wanted to see passed."

Amused, and with my interest rising, I sit on the bench beside her. "How did you answer?"

"Something about college football and the playoff system."

"Football, huh?" Very clever.

"I'm not really good at this politics stuff. I know enough to know when to keep my mouth shut about issues. That's about it." She thrusts the cupcake my direction. "Wanna bite?"

"Sure." I pinch off a piece, and jam it into my mouth, which elicits a smile from her. "The fact you suck at this whole thing is what people will love about you." I swallow the cupcake down and lean towards her. "Don't let them tame you, Tucker-Grace. Trust me. They'll manhandle you and try to stuff you into a cage so they can traipse you around for show. We're nothing more than circus animals brought into the ring as an act."

"And your dad's the ringleader."

Her assumption doesn't surprise me. "No. They use my dad as much as anyone. He's the main attraction."

She raises her eyebrows, and her brow crinkles in curiosity and confusion. "Then who?"

I could tell her it's big money donors, or bigwigs within the party, but I'm lying to her enough and have reached the point where continuing to lie is betraying an innocent soul.

She doesn't deserve any of this.

I'm staring into the eyes of someone that I hadn't even considered when I started playing the part of a spy. I didn't stop to think there would be casualties in our political war.

"My mom," I admit. "She's the one that wanted all of this."

Tucker-Grace reacts like a small bolt of lightning struck her. "Really?"

I turn, pull up one leg, and tuck it under the other so I can fully face her. "I think my dad could be happy as a small-town city-council member somewhere. As long as he's around people, he's happy. It's my mom that gets off on the power of it all."

Now she's the one who is studying me, and while her inspection causes a hitch in my heart rate, I don't break eye contact. I want her to read everything in me she can manage. Maybe she'll figure out things about me I haven't yet. Maybe she'll grow to trust me, even though we both know she probably shouldn't.

"You don't know me from Adam," she suddenly says. "Why would you tell me all of this?"

"Because I think I do know you."

She straightens her posture and looks back at the fire. I've momentarily lost her and not knowing where she travels in her mind, is frustrating. I want to know where she goes. I want to go with her.

"I thought you were angry with me," she blurts, catching me completely off guard.

"What?" I scoot towards her and try to read her face. "When?"

"When I got on the elevator." She returns from her mental trip and turns her face to me. "You glared at me."

"I glared?" I shake my head, knowing there's no way I would have reacted negatively to seeing her. She misread me. Many people do.

"I thought maybe you were upset by all the photos out there or something."

"First off, if I got upset every time there were pics of me scattered around the web, I'd be pissed twenty-four hours a day."

She looks back out at the fire. I've lost her again and panic sets in.

"It was your eyes," I admit, desperate to draw her back.

It works, and I'm relieved when she gives me her attention again. "My eyes?"

"Yeah. You've got these gold flecks, and your eyes looked more gold than green." I point to the outfit she's wearing. "I think it's the gold in the fabric that caused it." I'm being stupid and acting like a stalker. "I don't know. For some reason, it got my attention."

"It wasn't my brilliant personality?" she teases. The light of the fire dances of the gold flecks that now so often catch my attention.

"Well, that too."

We share a smile. I'm suddenly tongue-tied.

Out of the corner of my eye, I see Hyatt and Vinny simultaneously press their fingers to their earbuds. "Affirmative," they say simultaneously before moving closer to us.

"What's that about?" Tucker-Grace asks, with a head toss in their direction. "This place is so surrounded by security I can barely breathe. Like they suck up all the oxygen."

"They're here to protect you from me. Making sure I'm not violating you."

"Really?" She leans away and looks me over. "Do you defile girls often?"

I look down at my empty hands. "Not as often as I'd like." My eyes track back to hers, and I wait to see if she'll get the joke.

Playfully, she punches me in the arm. "Charming."

Relieved that she caught my sarcasm, I lean back onto my hands to stop the wringing, check out our security detail, and tap my foot against hers in an invitation to stand. "Want to get out of here?"

She shakes her head and smirks. "I'm not interested in being defiled, thank you very much."

"You think I'm like that?" There's genuine curiosity in my question. I want to know if she's totally bought in to the bad-boy image that's so easily thrown around the internet.

I anxiously wait for her response, although I don't quite understand why I need one so badly.

She looks down at the cupcake wrapper in her hands and

tosses it into the air, then catches it. Maybe it's a sign that she doesn't take all the rumors too seriously. It's not as heavy a topic as I might fear it is. "I think you like to act like you are," she finally says.

Relieved, I smile. She's better at all of this than she believes. Maybe I haven't thrown her into a storm completely helpless. "Yeah, you'll do just fine in the swamp." Standing, I offer her my hand. "Come on, I'll show you around. And you'll remain pristine. Pure as the driven snow, I promise."

The several seconds that Tucker-Grace stares at my hand and contemplate her response is an eternity, but I don't budge. My hand is hovering in front of her and offering a momentary escape from the madness, and I'm silently praying she'll take me up on the offer.

Tucker-Grace peers up at me with her green eyes and finally slips her hand into mine with a jingle of her bracelets. "I know karate," she warns as she stands.

"I'm sure you do."

Tucker-Grace looks over her shoulder at Hyatt and Vinny as we saunter toward the exit.

"You get used to it," I tell her, then turn to Hyatt and Vinny. "I got this, boys."

19

TUCKER-GRACE

Jack and I are in the middle of a speed round of *Ask Me Anything*, but we take a break here or there when we Jack points out the window at a site he wants to make sure I see. I can't tell if he just wants to give me a tour, or he's trying to convince me that this place isn't so bad.

Maybe he's figured out that I'm a skeptic to the core of my being. But, looking out across the area as we drive through the city, I have to admit he's right. Washington DC is impressive.

The history, buildings, and people. It's all stunning. And in the clothes I'm wearing, I belong. Like Cinderella, who transformed herself for the ball — I'm just not sure what time I'll turn back into the maid wearing the boring, dirty, shredded clothes.

A part of me wishes I'd spent more time in the nation's capital, but it never felt right, and I wonder if by some miracle Mom and Vice President Quaid win the election, if a place like Washington, DC could ever feel like home.

Jack and Fiona have made it work for them. Life as the children of a Congressman changing to that of the Vice President in DC had to have been quite a change, but Jack and Fiona have made it work for them.

He's sitting against the driver's side window in the back row of the SUV. I'm leaning against the passenger side window in the second. Our legs are laying across our seats and we're facing each other. The only light is from the street lamps and businesses outside the windows as we pass.

It's like we're punch drunk. Anything makes us laugh. The stress must've gotten to me, and this relief is good.

Real good.

"Do you dance?" I ask, still bubbling with a snicker about our last question.

He shakes his head. "Not at all. Snuggler or not a snuggler?"

"Never been a snuggler. Best pick up line?"

"Um..." He looks skyward, and I wait for a ridiculous response. When he finally looks back at me, he smirks. "I don't need any."

I burst out laughing again. "You're such a cocky bastard."

"It's true, though," he squeals, obviously embarrassed. "What do you want me to do? Lie to you?"

I shake my head and try to contain my laughter so I can continue with the game and learn more about him. "No. I hate liars."

He clears his throat. "Favorite pun?" he asks, quickly.

It takes a few seconds, but I pluck one from the back of my mind. "Why's the cookie sad?"

"I don't know." He shrugs. "Why?"

"Because his mom was a wafer long."

"That's so dumb." His head falls forward, over the back of my seat in a roar of laughs that make my soul feel good. There's something pretty amazing about making someone laugh. It's like you're giving each other a present.

Just as I start to ask another question, he laughs again, and I don't want to interrupt. He seems to need it as much as I do.

In a fit of snickers, he scoots back against the side armrest.

"What are your code names?" I ask.

He leans his head back against the window and sobers a bit. "My dad is Reaper. My mom is Regency. Fiona's Rosebud and I'm…"

"Do not say Romeo."

He wiggles a little in his seat.

"Jack Wright, if you say Romeo, I'm gonna come unhinged."

Guilt floods his face. "Why? What's wrong with Romeo?"

I'm mortified, by both the fact that it may be Romeo, and it may be Romeo, and I've embarrassed him. "No. Jack? Really?"

He grins. "No."

I'm beyond relieved. "Thank God. I'd lose all respect for you."

"I didn't realize you had any."

"What little I've conjured up. It would be gone. Turned to ash."

He swings his legs off the seat next to him and sits forward. "It's Roughneck."

It's a shocking revelation. Not at all what I'd expect from a boy from Pennsylvania. "Roughneck? As in Texas oil riggers? Those kinds of roughnecks?"

He nods, obviously embarrassed. "I was ten when we picked it. What can I say?"

I sit up and lay my arms over the back of the seat. "Why would you choose something so random?"

"I love history. I watch all those documentaries about how

the nation was formed. The Wild West, the land run. All of it fascinates me. Always has. I wanted to be a cowboy for a long time, but I'd never ridden a horse, and cowboy doesn't start with R, so I landed on Roughneck because they're bad ass. Hard workers. They've got a big job, and they just get it done."

"It suits you. A little rough around the edges, but when you dig down deep, you've got some substance."

"Am I the rigger or the oil in that scenario?"

I giggle again. "Both I guess."

He drapes his arms over my seat and rests his chin on his arm but keeps his eye contact which I'm growing accustomed to. It doesn't make me as uneasy as it did at first. Now, I expect it.

"It's not the name I wanted. I wanted Rawhide but couldn't have it because it was Ronald Reagan's call sign. Which is why I wanted it. They wouldn't let me copy it. And it's famous because when he was shot by Hinkley, they put the call out, 'Rawhide down'."

"Very dramatic." I never would've pegged him as a history buff. It's endearing. He's deeper than he gives himself credit.

"Is Reagan your political icon?" I ask.

"Absolutely. He was a hard-core capitalist and constitutionalist. A dreamer. He loved this country, and he wasn't afraid of pissing anyone off. He just did what he thought was best. And he did it in a completely cowboy sort of way. No fear."

I'm impressed and surprised by the way he talks about our former president and our country.

"I like that he saw the best in our country," he says. "You know? He didn't buy into all the negativity. I don't know what he'd think about where we are now. But I don't buy that everything's so bad. That this world is such a dark place and all we have left to do is hate each other because we have different opinions." He sighs. "Sometimes I wonder what he would do in this situation."

"I thought you hated politics."

"I hate the pettiness of politics. I hate the agendas and the narratives. But doing everything you can to better the country and protect what's good about it —that's what makes all the crap worth it."

Maybe he should be the one running for office. He'd have my vote. "Jack Wright, you're a romantic."

He lifts his head in surprise. "What?"

"A political romantic. You love the patriotic romantic parts of our history."

"Yeah."

"Did you ever get the horse ride?"

"Not yet." He rests his chin back down and stares past me out the window. I look over my shoulder to see what he's looking at. It's the Jefferson Memorial.

"Stop here at the park," he tells the driver, then slides to my side of the car. "We're at the Inlet Bridge. It's a well-known landmark in the area. From this park you can see the bridge and look out across the water at a perfect view of the Jefferson Memorial."

I turn around and press my forehead against the window, taking in the memorial lit up at night. "It's amazing."

"Want to get out and stretch your legs? We've got a while before the announcement."

"Sure." I should worry about my mother, and maybe I should even worry about Cody, but I'm not worried about either. If my mother wanted me, or was concerned about my whereabouts, she'd text.

Cody would too.

Vinny and Hyatt slide out of the vehicle first. Jack and I wait behind to give them time to survey the area.

"I'm gonna call your agent, Vampire Vinny," I say.

His laugh is back. "Vampire Vinny? Why?"

"His dark hair comes to a point on his forehead like old vampires do in movies." He'll take some getting used to. Luckily, I won't see him often after the announcement is made, and we go our separate ways to campaign. Or so my mother told me.

"Knock yourself out. I'm sure he'll love it."

Anywhere else, with anyone else, and I would consider our detail's behavior stalking. But in the here and now, it's necessary. And I hate it. "And I thought my aunt, Elliot, was bad."

"Once you realize that they don't interfere in anything you do, it's easier to get used to them."

That doesn't seem possible, but I'll take his word for it. "What about reporting back to our parents? Do they do that?"

"No." He climbs over the seat, into my row, and drapes his arm over the seatback behind me. "Why do you ask?" He leans towards me. "Do you plan on doing something you wouldn't want your mother to know about?"

I accept his challenge and stare into his eyes the way he stares into mine. It's not normal to maintain this much eye contact. It's intense. He can be intense, but not necessarily in a bad way.

My focus trails to his lips momentarily, but I force it back to his blue eyes. "Probably not." I break the connection and pull off the shoes that have been strangling my toes all night and exit.

"You know, you shouldn't be mad at her. She probably didn't even realize my dad had decided. And then it got leaked. It snuck up on her too."

"Maybe." Clutching the straps of my shoes in my hands, I step into the grass, and we start our walk. "No more about all that. I've sulked about it enough." I inhale the scent of freshly cut grass and then blow my remaining anger and hostility into the wind. "You're seventeen. A senior or a junior, the fact sheet didn't give your grade.

"I should be a senior, but I'll be a junior." He pulls his hands out of his front pockets. "My parents held me back the summer before the first grade. I couldn't sit still long enough."

That means the three of us are all juniors. Quite a coincidence. "Did holding you back help?"

"No. But playing the drums did. It gave me somewhere to channel all of that extra energy."

He's seemed so controlled since we've met. Other than fiddling with something in his hands from time to time, I've never noticed an inability to stay still. From what I've seen, he keeps focused extremely well.

"Drums really? Are you any good?"

He shrugs. "Some people think so. What about you?"

"No talents to speak of. I play a little tennis. That's about it, really."

"And you have a boyfriend."

The statement is out of nowhere. Has he been wanting to bring it up for a while? "An ex-boyfriend. At least this week. Our status changes like the direction of a tilt-a-whirl." Or a raging bull.

"Why is that?"

"Let's just say, I'm a little like you." I look up at his blue eyes, full of curiosity. "I can't sit still."

He smirks. "Good answer." He gently pulls me to a stop. "I like your thinking. Hold on." Jack kneels down on one knee, like he's about to propose with a big ol' diamond and then he's gonna promise to sweep me away from the mess if only I'll say yes.

But I stand as he unties his shoe.

Do his feet hurt like mine, or does he just like the feel of grass between his toes? I'll ask in our next round of Ask Me Anything.

"Back in the car you sounded like you have hope for the future of the country, but based on our dinner conversation, I take it you don't want our parents to win the election. Do you not agree with your dad's positions?"

He looks up at me with a squint. "Maybe it's a little self-ish. But in the eighties, someone did a study about the children of presidents." He slips his shoe and sock off and unties the second. "It showed that being related to a president brought more problems than positives."

My stomach churns. "Somehow that doesn't surprise me."

After removing his shoes and socks, he stands, and we continue walking. "More divorce. More alcoholism. Earlier death. Stuff like that. The worst of it is, they did the research before we had the Internet, social media, blogs, multiple twenty-four-hour news channels that have to have something to talk about and candidates to trash. Everyone wants to be the first to report something. Truth or fairness be damned."

I appreciate his honesty but want him to go against my belief in honesty at all times, lie to me and tell me all will be well if they somehow win.

He stops walking and stares at the Jefferson Memorial across the Inlet. I could follow his gaze but keep my eyes on him instead. "I imagine Thomas Jefferson and his family had it a lot better than modern day presidents and their offspring." When he looks back to me, my face flushes and wish I'd followed his gaze to Jefferson so I wouldn't have just been caught staring at him. Luckily, he didn't seem to notice.

"Don't get me wrong," he continues. "You'll have it good. Nobody pays the Vice President any attention. We went to the Thanksgiving turkey pardon the first year. That's about all they asked of us. We could walk into a store, and nobody even noticed."

The revelation is a relief. Obscurity sounds wonderful right about now. "But now you're everywhere. And, like I said earlier, everyone sees you as the bad boy. Not the guy I just got to know in the car."

Our hands briefly touch as we walk, sending an electrical pulse up my hand.

He grins down at me, and I catch my breath a little. Here, under the moonlight, he's beyond perfection, and with a mischievous look in his eye, he's trouble. For me, anyway.

"I play my part in the melodrama."

"Your part?"

"The more I'm up to, the less they mess with Fiona."

I'm surprised, and oddly relieved by his revelation. "So, you're protecting her?" Just like he wants to protect the country in his own way. It's chivalrous, really. In a time when chivalry is frowned upon.

By some.

"No. She can handle herself, but it's a lot."

"But not for you?"

He shrugs. "I don't internalize it or take it personally. I'm dead inside." He laughs, removes his suit jacket and lays it on the ground, then motions for me to sit.

I carefully sit so the jacket won't slide on the grass and leave a stain, and stare across the glistening water at Thomas Jefferson practically hidden inside a grand marble dome.

He sits down beside me but says nothing. Maybe we're both thinking about how big life seems and how out of control it feels.

"Jack, what does this mean for us?"

"What? The two of us being out here alone?" He's teasing, and I know it. It's sort of adorable.

"No." I reach over and slightly shove him away. "The campaign."

He extends his legs out in front of him and leans back on his elbows. "Once we lose… I guess we go back to normal."

I'm starting to think that normal isn't possible whether we win or don't. A lot has changed since I read the Twitter feed back at the lake and I'm not sure what I want anymore.

"Four hours ago, losing sounded like the right answer."

"And now?"

"It would devastate my mother. I don't want her to win, but I don't want her to lose her dream, either."

With my legs drawn to my chest and my chin on my knee, I look down at him. "Why are you so sure they'll lose?"

"A third-party candidate has never won the White House. Teddy Roosevelt was a former Republican who ran as an Independent and even he couldn't win."

If he'd told me that two hours ago, I'd doubt his knowledge, but he's proven himself to be well studied in a lot of things. History most importantly. He's a wise soul who has put a lot of thought into the ramifications of being the child of the president. "You really know your stuff."

"I'm not even sure I have a choice."

"In knowing all of this or the political life in general?"

"Either. Both. Does it matter?" He's now serious, and I wish we were back to laughing. When we talk about politics or the campaign, the weight of it is heavy.

He sits up. "Tell me about this ex-boyfriend of yours." Apparently, he was just as tired of being depressed as I was. "Specifically, why he's an ex." The levity to his voice has returned.

"He's not the most loyal sort."

"A serial cheater?"

I nod. "That... and he's got a temper."

He looks over at me with concern. "Violent?"

I shake my head, feeling guilty for the extreme character-ization of someone who is so often gentle and kind. "Not with me. He takes it out on the bulls." I look over at the memorial. "He's not a bad guy, he just isn't someone I can fully trust, and trust is the most important thing about a rela-tionship."

"Trust, yeah. I hear what you're saying." He looks up into the sky for a brief second. "What attracted you to him?"

"He wasn't scared of anything. I think a part of me wanted to be more like him and maybe some of him has rubbed off on me." I catch the odd wording and giggle. "In a non-literal way."

He snickers.

"But really, who knows what attracted me to him. I was fourteen when I first met him. And to be honest, I don't know what he found appealing about me, either. We're oil and water at times."

"Your independence?"

"No. I think he hates that sometimes."

"Your wit?"

"Usually he just thinks I'm giving him attitude, which I probably am."

"Uh... It could be your quick mind, or the awkward way you ramble when you're nervous."

I shake my head. "I'm not so sure about that."

"So, he hates you?" He laughs. "He hates everything about you."

I laugh along with him. "I guess so. What the heck am I doing wasting my time with him?"

"That's what I'm wondering." Jack leans back on to his elbows and fixes his eyes on me.

I match his posture and look up at the stars to avoid his gaze. The way his eyes suddenly seem to smolder is too alluring. "What about you? Dating anyone?"

"Nope."

"Anyone you want to date?"

"Nope."

With a shake of my head, I note the quickness of his answers. "Not even a hint of hesitation, Jack."

"Nope." He cackles, and I giggle like a girl with a wicked crush.

I give him my full attention once again. "At least you're honest. What about your sister?"

He tilts his head to the right but keeps his slate-blue eyes on me. "Single. I think. Why?" He smirks. "You interested?"

"Not this week."

"But you're single. This week."

I nod.

"And I'm single. Permanently." Jack turns onto his side, oozing school boy charm. "And we've both agreed that there's no way our parents will win this thing."

"Yes, we have."

"Once we lose, you and I will never see each other again."

"One can hope," I tease.

He looks away long enough to pick up a blade of grass and play with it in his fingers for a few seconds, but gazes right back over at me.

"You've gotta stop it with the eyes, Jack Wright."

His brow furrows. "What about my eyes?"

"Do you do that on purpose? Good lord."

He sits up and rests his elbow on his knee. "What are you talking about?"

"You said you can't sit still but you have this oddly amazing way of making eye contact at all times. Do you practice that?"

"I'm sure it's just you."

"That's noticed?" I shake my head. "No way."

"No. It's just you that holds my attention."

I swallow hard. My heart races and my head spins. I can't tell if he's full of crap and playing mind games, or he's sincere. *God, I hope he's being sincere.*

"Do girls buy the crap you shovel?"

His eyes widen in surprise, but the mischief remains. "Yes. I have a very high success rate."

I'm only half-sure he's teasing. "Trust me, Jack, they don't buy it. They pretend to so they can keep your attention."

"But you? You don't want to keep my attention?"

Even if I do, I'd never admit it to him. "The more interesting question is why would you want to give it?"

He answers without hesitation. "Because when I'm focused on you, the rest of the world fades away." He rests his head on his hand and props up on his elbow.

I gaze down at him, trying to read him. On the surface, he seems like an open book, but I'm sure he's got some hidden chapters.

"They say that what happens on the campaign stays on the campaign," he says, bringing my inspection to an end.

"Who's they?"

Jack shrugs. "I don't know. Who cares?"

He glances around, causing me to do the same, and half expecting a throng of people to be watching what could be an act, and if it is, it's a good one. "So, basically, it didn't happen."

I know exactly what he's alluding to but play coy. "What didn't happen?"

Jack leans towards me and waits. His eyes are nearly fire. "A campaign fling."

It sounds both fun and frightening. "Campaign fling? I'm not really the fling sort."

"Call it what you want." His eyes are smoldering in the light off the street lamps.

For some idiot reason, it's too much to resist. I lean to him, meeting him halfway. "What happens on the campaign, stays on the campaign."

Jack reaches over and strokes my cheek with his thumb with one gentle movement. When his lips softly touch mine, I lose all common sense.

I lower my head back to the ground as his kiss deepens.

Several seconds pass before I stop him. "This is ridiculous." I'm giggling and cover my face with my hands.

This isn't like me. Kissing a guy, the first day I met him is something I wouldn't normally do. I'd known Cody for years and gone out on multiple dates before I even held his hand.

I don't know why I'm so accepting of Jack's affection. He's not good for me. I believe this is a game for him. As he said, he's looking for a fling.

Maybe I am too. Or maybe it's nice to have someone's full attention, even if it's only for a while.

I peek through my fingers. Jack reaches down, grips my hands in his and pulls them away. "That's better," he whispers. "If you're going to laugh, at least let me watch."

"You don't find this insane?" I look up at him; my face is hot from embarrassment.

"Of course. That's what makes it so great." His hip rests

against mine, and his leg lies on the grass between mine. We seem to fit perfectly together.

"You're too charming."

He reluctantly lifts his head, causing my lips to cool in defiance. "What are we doing?" He sits up and shakes his head. Maybe he's hoping to shake some sense into it.

I lift off the ground onto my elbows and look over at him. My lips are slightly fuller from the friction. "This is what I'm saying. It's crazy. We should stop and head back. They're probably wondering where we are."

"If they want to find out where we went, they have two guys over there who can tell them in a few seconds."

He's referring to Hyatt and Vinny.

"And they won't tell them we're doing this?"

He shakes his head. "They aren't babysitters. Or spies."

He lays back down beside me, props back up on his elbow, and gazes at me, and I want to believe he's looking at me with honesty in his eyes, and this isn't a manipulation or act. "It may be crazy, Tucker-Grace, but I don't want to go back yet."

I throw all caution that I have left in my body to the wind. "Me either."

This time, it's me who leans toward him, nearly brushing my lips against his. But I stop and hover with nothing more than the width of a strand of hair to keep us apart.

He completes the bond. I place my hands on the back of his head and pull him back to me as I lay my head down on the grass. His kiss is intense but somehow tender.

I easily lose myself as his lips explore mine, and his fingers graze my neck.

Hyatt clears his throat, bringing us back to reality.

Jack groans, falling onto his back, and I'm embarrassed at being caught and cover my face with my hands again.

"I apologize for the interruption, but they need you back at the hotel for the announcement."

I uncover my face, sit up and look down at Jack with a grimace. "How long have we been out here?"

"Not long enough."

"Speak for yourself." I slip my shoes back on, stand, and offer Jack a hand. "Help you up?"

"How about I help you back down?"

I squat down and wrap my arms around my legs. "Thanks for taking my mind off things tonight. And for the laughs. I needed them."

Jack looks up at me. Sincerity fills his face, which I assume is a rare thing for him. "Any time. Especially what just happened. We can pick that right back up and-"

"Nice try, but that was a one-time thing." I stand back up, offer him my hand again, and when he takes it, pull him to his feet. "You know, what happens on the campaign stays on the campaign."

"Tucker-Grace, our campaign just started."

"Still, it's a one-night thing. After all, neither of us can sit still."

I turn to head back to the car but stop when Jack refuses to release my hand.

He tugs me back into his arms, kisses me, and I lose myself again.

20

FIONA

FUNDRAISER ATTENDEES ARE NOW multiple glasses of wine into the evening, the volume of the room and energy is through the roof.

Only a few more hours, and I will be free to reach out to Austin and try to help him, although I don't know how. His family is in a downward spiral, and all I'll be able to do is offer some emotional support and perhaps listen to him vent his anger or concerns.

Brittany and Pia are making it easier to distract myself. We're at the far end of the George Washington Terrace, near the back of the crowd, and they're drilling me for information about the campaign. They want to know if I've learned anything mind-blowing now that my father propelled further onto the world stage.

I find their interest intriguing. My father has been the Vice President for over six years. He's traveled the world, met with leaders around the globe, and they're suddenly, just now, tuned in to his every move.

And Jack.

They've asked a lot of questions about Jack, who is

nowhere to be found. He never takes these events as seriously as he should, but he's usually present and visible. His absence on such a big night will bring questions.

I assumed he left with a friend from school. Now that I see that Tucker-Grace has also disappeared from sight, it's obvious they've left together. I can only hope I'm the only one that's noticed.

They have been gone for quite some time. I left the room for less than thirty seconds and was immediately summoned back. We're held to different standards, and it's wholly unfair and infuriating, but I won't provide Pia and Brittany with even a hint of concern and interest. They won't get information out of me. My family and I only have each other, and I won't betray their trust in such a petty way.

For the first time since the event started, I'm relaxed and enjoying myself. Playing coy with my peers is entertaining, and they're so desperate for information; they humor my evasiveness.

"What about that redhead they spotted him with last night?" Pia asks.

I shrug. "Other than what I read on Grass Roots; I know nothing of her."

"What time did he get home last night? It had to have been late," she continues.

"Girls, I was asleep. I don't wait up to see what time he will come home every night."

"What about your mom?" Brittany asks, leaning towards me. "Josie is gorgeous. Does that make her nervous at all?"

The question catches me off guard and makes me uneasy. I hadn't even considered that my mother would give a second thought to Josephine's appearance or the chance that my father would notice. "No," I say, but don't truly know the answer. "It doesn't make her nervous at all."

"Well, what about Cody? Tucker's boyfriend. What do you know about him?" Pia asks.

"He's a bull rider and his family are wealthy, but that's all I know for now. I'm sure I'll find out more as the campaign progresses."

"Quit staring!"

My stomach flips. Recognizing the voice, I spin in my seat to see Austin at the entrance of the terrace, on his toes trying to see over the crowd as he shouts at the people in the room who are gawking at him.

It's anguish to see him so lost and desperate.

His black hair is disheveled, and he hasn't shaved in a few days. Stubble covers his face. The red of his eyes makes his blue eyes stand out as he searches the room.

I freeze. My face heats and my fingers curl around the back of the ladder-back chair. I search the room and find Mother, surrounded by donors and watching Austin move through the room.

"How did he get an invitation?" Brittany whispers.

"He's drunk," Pia says, disgusted. "Or high. Look at him. He can't stand up straight."

"We've been right all along. Like father, like son," Brittany adds.

Secret Service agents on the perimeter of the patio have their eyes on him but stay back. They won't move unless he does something, or my father asks them to remove him. This is far from the first time someone became inebriated at a campaign event and the girls acting outraged is for show. They see students from our school drunk at parties all the time.

Austin continues to bulldoze his way through the partygoers, knocking drinks out of people's hands, and pushing them into one another. In a matter of moments, he'll spot me, and there's a chance he'll make a larger scene. I need to leave the room but can't force myself away.

I remain stunned and silent. Pia and Brittney take in the spectacle with awe and warped pleasure because there is nothing like seeing one of your own fall from grace. It makes good gossip.

Austin and I somehow make eye contact. I sense his desperation as he heads my way, and afraid he'll say something, jump to my feet and rush towards the exit, escaping out the side entrance.

I enter the hallway and quickly walk away from the terrace to lead him away from the crowd.

"Fiona, wait!"

I have to force words through my constricted throat. "What are you doing here?" My voice is shaky.

"I needed... I needed..." He slurs his words. "I needed to see you."

I look over my shoulder. Lana is only a few steps behind, and her stride matches his. I don't normally fear Austin but given the circumstances of his drunkenness combined with his anger, anything is possible. Even violence.

"We promised to use discretion," I say. "Busting into a campaign event is not discretion." If word gets out that he crashed my father's announcement drunk, to see me, this will cause a firestorm among blogs and online magazines.

"Screw discretion. Everything is falling apart. My family, my mom's health — all of it."

This is horrible for him, but I still can't condone his showing up on such a special night. "Why come here?"

"I wanted to see my girlfriend is that-"

"Shh..." I spin around and put my hand out, pushing him to a stop. "You need to leave. Now."

"Fiona, I'm moving away. We'll hardly see each other. We-"

"It's probably for the best," I say, willing myself to become indifferent.

It's a tactic I've come by easily. Possibly from being abandoned as a child. The older I get, the more easily I shut down my emotions, and I've become so good at it, it frightens me.

"For your family, I mean," I add, forcing compassion to win out. "You need time to heal, and the campaign is ramping up, so I'll have more responsibilities. I can't afford to-"

"Be seen with the bastard son of a US Senator mired in scandal." Austin finishes the sentence.

Mired in scandal. It's a term often used by journalists when they refer to his father.

Austin is obviously defeated and heartbroken. My rejection is a final insult to injury. He drops his head. The burden is too large. "I get it."

Regret floods over me as he walks away. I was too cold.

He swings his arm and knocks a vase off a nearby table, sending it crashing to the floor.

I shiver at the sound and sight of shards of glass falling to the floor.

He walks further and destroys another vase of flowers before exiting the hallway.

"Ladies and gentlemen, please head into the Grand Corcoran Ballroom..." An announcer is speaking over the loudspeaker.

I sigh, void of the will to walk back into the crowd and pretend that all is more than well.

"... for an exciting announcement."

The crowd erupts in cheers, snapping me back into the moment. My parents need me. My personal drama can wait.

I raise my head, prepare to return to the patio, and follow the guests into the ballroom.

I spin around and nearly run into Lana. "Your father would like to speak with you. He knows about Austin's outburst."

With no energy left to argue, I lower my head, nod, and follow Lana down the hall.

I cannot formulate a plan of what to say because I don't know what my father knows. This could be a simple request to get my friends under control, or he could know about my relationship with Austin.

If he knows, this conversation will be an uncomfortable one.

When Lana ushers me into a small room, I find Austin sitting at the table under the watch of Agents Mayfield and Pearce. Austin's hunched over, his eyelids are half closed, and he's sweating profusely.

He's broken. I want to reach out and comb his hair away from his eyes like I so often do.

The door opens. I startle. My neck tightens.

My father walks into the room and takes a cold look at Austin before turning his disappointment to me. "You invited this boy here?"

I shake my head. "He came with Pia."

I'm fully focused on my father. Nothing hurts more than disappointing him. I'll say and do anything to avoid it.

He turns back to Austin. "You're Lee's boy."

Austin nods.

"I suppose it's been a rough day." I'm relieved by his compassion. My father is a truly kind man who rarely has the opportunity to show just how much.

Austin keeps his eyes on the table. "Yes, sir," he mutters.

My father looks to Agent Pearce. "Take him to the entrance of the hotel and don't allow him back inside."

"Yes, sir." Agent Pearce looks at Austin. "Let's go."

Reluctantly, Austin pushes his chair back, stands, and follows Agent Pearce out the door without a glance my way. I follow behind, hoping to escape further questions from my father.

"Fiona. A word, please."

My blood runs cold, and I stop following Austin, remain in the room, and close the door back.

"I suppose I don't have to tell you that will never happen again."

My heart aches. "No, Sir. It won't."

He takes a step towards me. "I don't know what it is you're doing with that boy, but it will stop." He whispers the words as if he's worried everyone in the hotel will hear them. "Immediately. Do you understand?"

I swallow hard and nod.

"Do you understand?" he repeats, more directly.

"Yes, Sir." I wait for him to leave before regaining my composure and walking out of the room.

I return to the terrace and move through the crowd to reach Austin to ensure that he leaves the premises without causing more trouble.

"Fiona!"

A girl in her early teens approaches from my right, but I pretend not to see or hear her, and move across the terrace with the crowd.

"Fiona!" The girl shoves towards me. "Can I get a selfie?"

What I want to tell her is that it is the worst time. I'd like to tell her I don't owe her a photo and if I refused to give one, that wouldn't make me a horrible person. I'd like to ask her to not think of herself for a moment. I want someone in my life —or even outside of it, to stop being selfish and stop asking for so much.

But I can't say any of those things.

Unable to deny seeing her any longer, I stop and force a smile. "Of course."

"Thank you," the girl squeals as she jumps up and down. "I just love you so much!"

I search the terrace for Austin, who is nowhere to be found. Hopefully, they quietly removed him from the hotel. "I appreciate that."

Compelled to honor the girl's request, I drape an arm over her shoulder and smile wide as she takes the photos.

"Have a great rest of your evening," I tell her before walking away.

I lightly push through the people and walk down the hall in the opposite direction of the crowd, knowing Lana is close behind. After turning a corner, I stop, remove my shoes, and run towards the main entrance.

When Lana and I arrive outside, Jack and Tucker-Grace are climbing out of an SUV and watching an angry Austin stumble around near the entrance.

"Austin, please go," I beg.

Immediately subdued by the sound of my voice, Austin staggers to me. "I just wanted to say I'm sorry."

Tears fill my eyes as I step toward him. "You shouldn't have to come to the biggest night of my father's life to do that."

Austin pulls his car keys from his pocket and fumbles with them in his hand.

Jack bounds toward him, trying to yank the keys from his grip. "Austin, dude, this isn't smart. Let's get you home."

"Home?" Austin chuckles, so obviously disgusted with

the term. He takes a step towards Jack and Tucker-Grace and raises his fists, ready to swing.

I look to the agents who move in. If Austin acts, they'll jump on him before he can make contact.

"Home? What is that?" he cries.

Cautiously, I walk up to Austin before the agents do. If I don't de-escalate the situation, our detail will have no choice but to act. "We can discuss this later. Please go. Sleep this off, and we'll discuss it tomorrow."

Austin grips me by the arm. Jack physically separate us. "Back off." He looks over his shoulder at Tucker-Grace. "Stay back," he tells her.

Agent Pearce closes in.

Tucker-Grace backs away and reaches for my hand as she goes. I instinctively accept the offer and together we move away as Austin takes a drunken swing at Jack.

On full alert, Jack leans to his left, missing the jab. Secret Service agents rush in. Agent Pearce contains Austin's flailing arms.

I can't believe what I'm witnessing. My hands are shaking. I search the area for any signs of media or paparazzi but don't see the flash of cameras.

"Austin, please go," I beg. "Please. If you don't leave, they'll arrest you." His arrest would only be more fodder for a starving press core.

"I'm sorry," he mutters, his energy zapped.

"I know," I whisper.

"I love you."

I look to Jack, afraid to see his reaction to Austin's declaration. His jaw drops. "What the-?"

Without responding to my brother's reaction, I lightly touch Austin's arm. "But please, go." I look to Lana. "Please, just let him go."

"He's drunk, Fiona. We can't let him drive."

"I'll - I'll…" Jack shakes his head, possibly sobering up to the fact that Austin, and I are dating. "I'll get him a ride." Jack pulls his phone out of his pocket and types on it, before turning the screen to me so I can see he's just ordered a Lyft.

With things calmed, I look around. I'm holding Tucker-Grace's hand. The girl I just met witnessed the entire chaotic and embarrassing event.

My limbs turn rigid. Shame fills my body. I drop Tucker-Grace's hand and back away.

Jack hands Vinny his phone. "Here, a car is on the way. Get him out of here before my dad does something."

The agent leads Austin away, leaving Jack and me to exchange a look between us. He looks bewildered by the chaos. I shake my head. A silent plea for him to leave discussion for later.

Tucker-Grace steps forward. "Trust me, I understand. It's complicated."

"You understand nothing," I snap, angry that someone from the outside witnessed the demise of our relationship.

I straighten my dress, smooth out the wrinkles, slip on my shoes. I only have to make it another hour, and then I'll be free to go home and fall apart in private.

Just another hour.

I walk back inside as if nothing happened.

The rumble of an electric crowd inside the large ballroom travels throughout the hotel.

When Jack, Tucker-Grace, and I approach the ballroom, Skip stops us before we walk through the door. "Are you three ready?"

I see Jack and Tucker-Grace nod, then copy their movements with a nod of my own, even though even with my best effort, I'm not ready.

On command, staffers fully open the door, and we walk inside and to the side of the stage to join my mother.

Wright/Bishop banners and signs fill the room, and an electric excitement hangs in the air like the thousands of red, white, and blue helium-filled balloons that hover around the ceiling.

The celebration is a sign that my parents have raised the political capital and endorsements necessary to make a viable run for the presidency. Not only are the people in the room excited about the possibilities, they're hopeful for a bright and more united future.

"Where have you been?" my mother whispers with a smile still on her face, which reminds me to smile.

"To borrow a quote, it's complicated." Jack and my mother share a look, and she doesn't ask any further questions.

Wait staff distribute champagne flutes filled to the rim to all the adults in the room. They told us teenagers would receive sparkling cider, but I could use the champagne.

"... To all of you, who share our passion for uniting this country and bringing it back to its full glory, I say: join us," Josephine says from the stage.

My mother straightens her back and allows her arms to hang limply at her side. She appears relaxed, but I'm not sure.

Were Pia and Brittany correct, and my mother is bothered by Josephine being on the ticket because it will require her to be near my father.

Does my mother ever fear he will stray? And if she does, is it a new fear, or one that is familiar?

"... For the sake of not only our present lives but the future of our children and grandchildren. And even their grandchildren. Join us and let's unite this country under our next President of the United States of America — Quaid Wright."

The crowd erupts. My father steps onto the stage, walks to Josephine, takes Josephine's hand in his and lifts their clasped hands into the air in a show of victory.

Patriotic music plays overhead as my mother, Tucker-Grace, Jack, and I join the candidates on stage for the grand finale.

Balloons and confetti fall from the ceiling. Amid a red, white, and blue shower, I see Tucker-Grace and Jack share a glance and a small smile before Tucker-Grace looks to me. Unlike her and my brother, Tucker-Grace and I do not exchange friendly smiles.

As I look back out at the crowd, cameras flash, and a tumultuous journey begins.

21

JACK

It's a few minutes after sunrise, and my parents and I are pulling on to the tarmac. Tucker-Grace and her mother are in the car behind ours.

I'd hoped that Tucker-Grace and I could ride in the same vehicle, but we left our residence, and she departed from the Four Seasons, so we got no more time together.

After the kiss at the park, we walked straight into a fight and then a celebration. We never got another second alone.

I don't know how she feels about our time together. Or about me.

It was a torturous night of tossing, turning, and hoping I didn't blow it with her on the first night. I got in my own way again.

I hope Tucker-Grace doesn't feel like she paid the price.

The SUV comes to a stop. My parents exit the vehicle first and take their time doing it. By the time I make it out behind them, Tucker-Grace is already halfway to the airplane and showing no signs she'll divert and head our way.

It's disappointing.

Josie approaches my dad and extends her hand for a

shake. "Thank you so much for such an amazing day. Tucker-Grace says thank you." She looks over her shoulder at her daughter. "She's a little worn out."

"I'm sure she is," my mom tells her, with a polite smile.

My parents lead her towards the plane, leaving Tanner and I leaning against the SUV as they say their goodbyes.

Tucker-Grace ambles and nearly drags herself up the stairs. Not that I can blame her, we threw her into a whirlwind, and it spit her out the other side.

"Five bucks says she looks back at me."

"You're on," Tanner answers.

My heart races as the anticipation mounts, and I wait for the moment that Tucker-Grace turns and takes one last look at me before she heads inside the plane.

If she does, it'll be a sign that she's at least somewhat interested.

She stops on the top riser, ducks inside, and disappears without looking back. My heart sinks.

"You owe me." Tanner sounds ecstatic that Tucker-Grace didn't give me another second of attention. "But don't fret, maybe Ava is still available. I'm sure I can track down her number."

I keep my eyes on the plane as he walks away.

She'll return to the door and wave goodbye, or at least glance my way.

"… I'm up for the challenge," Josie is saying her goodbyes to Dad and Mom a few feet away. "… and looking forward to uniting the country."

Josie heads towards the plane, but I focus on the windows.

"Come on, Tucker-Grace," I mutter, refusing to give up.

Josie reaches the top step, turns and waves one last time before she disappears into the plane.

A window shade raises. My heart thuds in my chest when Tucker-Grace peers out the window, searching the tarmac.

Her eyes finally meet mine, and she smiles.

I've somehow captured Tucker-Grace's attention and oddly, doing so makes me believe I can take on the world. And win.

"Why didn't you inform me he would announce tonight?" Sheldon approaches and leans against the SUV beside me, but I keep my eyes on Tucker-Grace as the electrical charge of the unspoken moment between us melts away.

My jaw tenses. "It was sudden," I manage through gritted teeth. "Didn't get a chance."

"The President wasn't happy being sideswiped like that. The Josie news was supposed to sink his campaign. Now they'll be riding high."

I shrug. It isn't my concern.

"This campaign needs to fail before it catches fire," Sheldon continues. "Full steam ahead, Jack. Make the President happy and continue feeding us information, or we'll leak everything."

I watch Tucker-Grace through the window as the plane pulls away. When I lose sight of her, the world crashes back in, and I'm reminded of what I'm up against.

"Stick with the plan," Sheldon says before walking away.

I weigh my options, knowing that I only have two. I can continue sharing what I know and risk my life imploding. Or, I can stop sharing information and still watch my life implode. Both options suck, and I'm between a hammer and the anvil.

Even if my father becomes the next President of the United States, for me, there is no winning.

When Tucker-Grace disappears from sight, I open my Instagram account, find her account, and follow it.

THE HOUSE IS QUIET, and the lack of noise is unsettling.

The televisions are off, the house staff is busy on the upper floors, and Lana is in the back of the house catching up on paperwork.

Everyone else has gone to the airport to see Josephine and Tucker-Grace off — including Jack.

Given the way they were looking at each other last night on the stage, something is brewing, and the percolating relationship has me nauseous. It doesn't settle well. Something is off.

I pick up my teacup and take a sip, hoping the green tea and honey will sooth the queasiness in my stomach.

Holding the teacup in both hands, and with one foot on the chair, I stare at my phone laying on the table and wonder if I should reach out to Austin or leave well enough alone.

I did the right and difficult thing by ending it with him. His behavior, my upcoming responsibilities, and my father's demand that I not see him again have provided me with the perfect excuse to keep a distance from one another.

While I may not have handled it as delicately as one

might hope, we need to free one another from the strain that our secret relationship brings.

I reach out and flip the phone over, so I no longer see the screen and continual alerts of Austin's persistent attempts to apologize for his behavior.

Increasingly unnerved by the silence in the residence, I retrieve the remote controls from the middle of the table and turn on the four televisions in the room, and mute all but one.

Six "political contributors" are discussing my father's event from the night before.

"But will Josephine Bishop be enough to give the Wright candidacy the boost it needs to receive an invitation to take part in debates?" a woman asks.

"No."

"Possibly."

"Yes."

I mute the television. Their experts are as clueless as anyone else.

In reality, we need a perfect storm. A daring contingency of voters willing to rage against the establishment. A message that will appeal across all aisles. A campaign that reaches beyond the media and meets the people where they are. And for no scandals to plague the re-birthed campaign.

My phone vibrates on the table again. I turn it over and check the message. It's from a blocked number.

Perhaps Austin is trying a new tactic. Reaching out through a phone number I don't recognize.

I open the message and find a photograph of Jack and Tucker-Grace at the Inlet Bridge standing in an embrace and kissing.

My stomach seizes and my chest tightens. *So reckless. So stupid.*

In less than twenty-four hours, my brother and this girl

have already put the entire campaign in jeopardy. If the world finds out that they were making out on the night of the announcement, all attention will shift away from the message and onto discussions about Jack and Tucker-Grace. We will lose the momentum that the announcement of a Vice Presidential candidate is supposed to give.

Lana walks into the room. "Here. Advance copy." She drops a magazine onto the table in front of me. On the cover, a split image of Tucker-Grace and me, with the headline: Will these young women be... THE PRESIDENTS' DAUGHTERS?

The queasiness in my stomach returns like a tidal wave. All eyes are now on us, and she is far too unpredictable to handle the pressure.

The phone vibrates again. After another sip of tea, unable to resist the urge, I turn the phone back over to the message illuminating on the screen. I'm sorry. Please, let's talk.

"Can I get you anything else?"

I look up at the chef and force a smile. "No. I'm wonderful. Thank you."

He leaves the room, I'm alone again, and there is only one thing that will cure the ache in my soul.

I stand, pick up the phone, and walk towards the front door. "I'm going for my run."

Lana walks into the entryway, dressed and ready to follow.

I put my earbuds in, turn on my running playlist, and step outside into the warm air as I type a message to Austin.

Meet me at the track.

* * *

Want more Fiona, Tucker-Grace, and Jack?

Pre-order Episode Two: *Familiar Ways*, now!

AND

Join us over on Grassroots.Fashion
were we get a glimpse of the fashion and lifestyle from the
series, have a fan forum, and more!

ALSO BY STEFNE MILLER

Losing Brave

(with Bailee Madison)

Collision

Salvaged Series

(Salvaged and Rise available in one book)

52658659R00093

Made in the USA
San Bernardino, CA
08 September 2019